Charles Wesley Alexander

The Career and Adventures of John H. Surratt

Charles Wesley Alexander

The Career and Adventures of John H. Surratt

ISBN/EAN: 9783337330224

Printed in Europe, USA, Canada, Australia, Japan

Cover: Foto ©Andreas Hilbeck / pixelio.de

More available books at **www.hansebooks.com**

THE CAREER AND ADVENTURES

OF

JOHN H. SURRATT,

SINCE HIS FLIGHT FROM AMERICA,

AFTER THE EXECUTION OF HIS MOTHER, MRS. MARY SURRATT,. PAYNE, HAROLD, AND ATZEROTT FOR THE ASSAS- SINATION OF PRESIDENT LINCOLN.

His Enlistment in the Pope's Zouaves in Italy—His Betrayal by his Mistress to U. S. Minister King—His Arrest and Desperate Escape—His Flight to Egypt, aided by Brigands whose Band he had Joined,

HIS FINAL ARREST

IN EGYPT BY UNITED STATES CONSUL HALE.

PHILADELPHIA:
PUBLISHED BY C. W. ALEXANDER,
224 SOUTH THIRD STREET.

JOHN H. SURRATT,

THE CONSPIRATOR.

It has been a year and a half since the assassination of President Lincoln startled and shocked the community, and nearly that long since the conspirators by whose hands he died, and who intended to complete their bloody work by the murder of the whole Cabinet at Washington, received their punishment. All were captured save one, and that one was John H. Surratt.

This miserable man was the son of Mrs. Mary E. Surratt, who was hung, together with Payne, Harold, and Atzerott, for a crime of which her son John was undoubtedly the principal plotter. Surratt, who, at the time of his capture, was twenty-eight, was born in Maryland. In his early years he was an exemplary young man, so conducting himself as to win the esteem of all who knew him. In appearance he is rather striking, his height being fully five feet ten inches, his build spare but muscular. His forehead is full, his eyes deep and bright, his mouth firm and rather small. His nose is large, and his hair, which is light in color, is long and wavy. He generally wore a heavy moustache and imperial, which gave him quite a fashionable appearance.

To his other bad qualities, Surratt adds that of the most abject cowardice. For, when he found that all was discovered, and that his mother—she who had borne him, who loved him—was to be hung like a common felon, if he had had one spark of filial affection, or one grain of manhood, he would have hastened to her, and died with her on the same scaffold.

Instead of that, he fled like a craven to Canada, received from the Confederate agents there his share of gold, and then, after hiding until the Summer grass was beginning to wither on his mother's grave, he sailed for Europe to enjoy his money. But enough of comments—all we could say would not increase the detestation which even a Southerner must have for such a man.

According to the partial confessions made by Surratt, he and John Wilkes Booth originally made up a plot, with the assistance of Payne and one or two others, to capture President Lincoln, on the occasion of the latter's inauguration, March 4th, 1865. But the officers in charge of that ceremony so effectually guarded against any such danger, that the conspirators found it impossible to attempt the consummation of their design.

Enraged at their non-success, they at once renewed their plotting; and this time with a far deadlier intent than before. And among themselves they swore a solemn oath to deliberately murder Mr. Lincoln, Mr. Johnson, General Grant, and Secretaries Seward, Stanton and Chase. The time fixed upon for the execution of the deed was April 14th, 1865. On the 5th or 6th of the same month, John H. Surratt went to Canada, doubtless for the purpose of procuring more money from Jacob Thompson, who held credits in the name of the Confederate States to an immense amount. He was at Montreal; and thither Booth wrote to Surratt to return instantly to Washington, that he might be on hand to take his part in the assassination. He did start the next day; but apparently from a desire to shift all the active part of the work upon his companions in guilt, and thus secure his own safety and reward at the same time, he delayed, from place to place, until he heard of the assassination being accomplished. Thereupon he immediately took the returning train to Canada, disguising himself, and assuming the name of Hamson.

Yet, with all his cunning, Surratt seems to have been, to use a very homely phrase, cat-witted; for at the hotel table in St. Albans, Vermont, he chanced to be drawn into conversation with a gentleman, to whom he actually boasted of having once, in connection with John Wilkes Booth. made the effort to "*capture Abe Lincoln, and run him off to Richmond.*" This referred, of course, to the original plot for the inauguration day. The gentleman thereupon took from his pocket a newspaper, and read a detailed account of the terrible affair. Surratt was astonished to find his own name mentioned in this account. He immediately took alarm, left the room, and going to a stable, hired a buggy—took a boy with him to bring it back— and then drove up the turnpike to a station fifteen miles away, where he boarded a train that was going north. He never stopped a single moment until he was safely across the dividing line at Rouse's Point.

Once in Canada, Surratt breathed a little more freely, but not much, for, to his dismay, he learned from a friend—at whose house he had often, during the rebellion, put up while carrying dispatches for the Confederate agents—that several daring American detectives had laid a plan for capturing Beverly Tucker, Thompson, and Sanders, and carrying them bodily across the boundary into the jurisdiction of the United States. He at once set out for Montreal, and secured rooms at St. Lawrence Hall, a hotel kept by J. Hogan, a man who was ardent in his friendship for the rebels, and through whose manœuvres Surratt, under half a dozen different names and in as many disguises, was enabled to remain at liberty, in spite of the efforts to take him, until the very moment he started for the steamer which was to carry him to Europe. The *alias* he used now was McCarthy. This was in September.

Once clear of the American shore, Surratt seemed to lose considerable of his caution; and before he had reached Londonderry he imparted to Mr. B——, a gentleman with whom he had struck up an acquaintance, a full history of himself—in fact, so complete that Mr. B—— asked him, plainly:

"What is your right name? Is it not Surratt? You have told me more than any man, save John H. Surratt, could have told me."

"Yes," replied the conspirator, "I am the identical John H. Surratt, but I am safe from all danger now."

The gentleman said nothing; but when he landed he hastened to United States Consul Wilding, at Liverpool, and told that official all that had passed on board the steamer.

"Mr. B——," said Mr. Wilding, "if you will give me your affidavit to this matter, I will forward it to the United States Minister at London, Mr. Adams, and you will doubtless receive a very handsome reward."

"I will with pleasure make the required affidavit," said Mr. B——, "but my conscientious scruples will not allow me to take any reward for merely doing my duty."

The affidavit was made at once, and sent to Mr. Adams.

Mr. Wilding, in addition, wrote to Secretary Seward himself, detailing the circumstances of the case. After waiting until October, Consul Wilding received a communication from Mr. Adams, in which the latter said that he did not consider it desirable, with their present evidence of identity and complicity, to apply for a warrant of arrest for the supposed Surratt.

About this time the conspirator ascertained what was going on, and once more changed his name—this time to Ingersoll—and adopted the disguise of an old man. Thus he made his way to London, where, taking apartments in a street in Piccadilly, he advertised in the London *Times*, for a young man to be a companion to an invalid gentleman. From among the numerous applicants he selected one who, he judged from his appearance, would be the most serviceable to him. The man's name was Hendrickson, seemingly a poor, timid fellow of about twenty; thin, but wiry, with a half silly countenance, which expression was rendered more so by the fact that his eyes were badly crossed. Hendrickson was duly installed in his new position, and, as he recovered his confidence, he became decidedly useful to his master. In fact, he was so much so, and displayed at times such quickness of perception and curiosity to know things, that Surratt began to suspect that after all, instead of having hired a good-natured simpleton, he had taken into his employ either a detective, or an exceedingly shrewd man.

Once this idea got possession of the fugitive conspirator, he was not long in determining on another secret flight, and leaving his valet quietly behind. As we have said, Surratt was an adept at disguising himself; and on this occasion he well sustained his character for ability in this direction.

One afternoon Hendrickson asked leave of his master to pay a visit to his mother, which Surratt was only too willing to grant, as it would afford himself the opportunity which he so much desired. The moment the valet had gone, Surratt sprang from the cushioned and pillowed chair in which he usually reclined, locked the door, threw off his dressing-gown, flung down his wig of gray hair, and stretched himself, with a grim smile of satisfaction.

"Ah! Johnny Hendrickson, my innocent ferret," said the conspirator, soliloquizing, "when you come back from seeing your mother, you will not find the poor, sick old man, though he will leave you his old clothes."

While he thus talked, Surratt was busy divesting himself of his disguise and replacing it with another—that of a fashionable London swell, which he chanced to have in his trunk. By the time he had completed the change, Johnny Hendrickson himself would not have been able to recognise him. The fugitive had two trunks, and from them he carefully removed his valuable papers and one or two other articles, and then lighting a cigar, he boldly left his room, from which, since first coming to the house, he had until this moment never stirred. He encountered the landlady, bustling about the hallway; but she bestowed on him nothing but a glance, taking him, doubtless, for a visitor, a fast nephew perhaps of the poor sick gentleman. As may readily be supposed, Surratt, chuckling at his good fortune, made no attempt to make himself known, but passed out into the street.

The streets of London afford a refuge from detection to fugitives, the security of which can hardly be conceived; and Surratt was well aware of the fact. For once out of sight of his lodging-house, it would be easier to find a particular fish in the ocean than to find him, especially in his present disguise. Hardly knowing or caring whither he directed his steps, he strode along until he began to feel hungry, when he turned aside into a cook-shop. Here he purchased a mutton-chop and some slices of bread, which he carried to a neighboring beer-shop, and calling for ale, sat down to his repast. As he laid his meat and bread upon the little table at which he sat down, the sounds of a familiar voice struck upon his ear; and looking across the room, he saw his valet, Johnny Hendrickson, in close conversation with a strange looking man, who did but little talking, but a great deal of listening. Hendrickson now had no crossed eyes!

" I tell you," said Johnny, " there's somethin' werry queer about that old gent. He's just the rummest chap as ever I clapped eyes on !"

" Does he ever have any visitors ?" asked the strange looking man.

" He's never had one from the first day I took service with him," replied Johnny; " but there's somethin' queer about him, I can tell you, and you'd better send a man down to watch him."

The conversation between the two went on thus for fully twenty minutes, during which time both often cast glances at Surratt. He never for a moment, however, showed any signs of paying attention to their conversation ; but while he ate he listened eagerly, so as not to lose a single word of what was said.

Presently Hendrickson rose, and said to his companion :

" Well, I've put you on the track now, and you can follow it up if you like. But mind, don't forget me when the reward comes ; that's all. I must be off, for the old fellow'll be gettin' cranky by the time I get back."

"All right," said the other, whom Surratt took to be a Bow-street detective, "all right, I'll see that he's piped, [a slang word for watched;] and if I find enough cause to pull [arrest] him, why you'll share, you know."

With this both went out of the ale-house, Hendrickson passing so close to Surratt as to brush his clothes.

"Ah ha ! my dear valet," smiled Surratt to himself, " you will find your aged, crippled old master *non est* when you return, and you will wait some time, I am very sure, ere you see him again."

After finishing his meal, the fugitive left the tavern, and calling a hackney-coach, had himself driven to the other extremity of London, where he found no difficulty in securing an apartment in an obscure locality, at a cheap rate. Here he lived for some time, wandering about the streets in daytime, and procuring his meals at cook-shops and taverns, and sleeping in his room at night. When it is recollected that the conspirator took with him from America at least ten thousand dollars in gold exchange, it will be easily seen that he had no need to work.

Yet, like any fugitive from justice, Surratt soon began to tire of his present kind of life, and he determined to go to Paris and enjoy the excitements of that gay capital. Hitherto he had lived very close as regarded expenditures, and consequently, of his ill-gotten gains he had still the greater portion left. So to Paris he started, secure in his disguise ; for, by way of testing it, he had on several occasions stopped rebel friends who previously knew him well, to ask the names of streets, or to light his cigar, and never had one of them recognized him.

SURRATT FLEES TO PARIS.

At the passport-office he got his passport in the name of Harvey, and soon afterward was crossing the channel to Calais. Here his papers were *vised* by the proper official, and *Harvey* took his seat in the conveyance for that Babylon city of Europe, the capital of France, which in due time he reached. Here he made himself known to three Southern men whom he knew he could trust with his terrible secret, and was by them introduced as Mr. Harvey, from England, to a circle of boon companions.

Surratt—or, as he now called himself, Harvey—quickly entered upon a course of dissipation. As a consequence, it was not long ere he made the acquaintance of a dashing and fashionable woman, with whose winning ways he was at once captivated. This woman's name was Louise Le Grande, and she fully returned the ardor of Harvey's passion. The next consequence was, that the conspirator's gold began to melt away like snow under the beams of a Spring sun; and after consorting with Louise for about six months, Harvey found himself possessed only of about a thousand dollars.

During a moment, too, of inadvertence, the fugitive had confessed to his mistress who he really was; and he dreaded that if he should break off his connection with her, she would betray him, and thus endeavor to obtain the large reward which the United States Government had offered for his apprehension. He would quickly have changed his disguise, and fled from the city; but a fearful fascination, that mysterious link which binds man to woman—more so, even, in vice than virtue—prevented the execution of his wish.

One night he and Louise had returned from the opera, and were sitting together in their apartment, when suddenly he noticed her casting furtive glances at the door. She also began to consult her watch every few moments, and seemed much perturbed about something.

"What is the matter, Louise?" asked Surratt, endeavoring to appear composed, but with the blood rushing through his veins like a liquid torrent of fire.

"Oh! nothing, sweetest, nothing at all. You must be very nervous!"

"Then why do you yourself seem so nervous? You never did so before. You look at the door, and then at your watch, and then look at the door, as though you had made an appointment with some one."

"Well, and if I had, what of it? That can be nothing to you," replied Louise, with a kind of mischievous glance.

"But it is a great deal to me!" sharply retorted Surratt. "For you know that I love you better than any one else in the world, and would never brook a rival."

CARDINAL ANTONELLI,

(From an Imperial Photograph,)

Prime Minister of the Papal Government, who so promptly arrested Surratt,
who, under the name of Watson, was serving in the Zouave battalion.

"*Mon Dieu!* my love, what a jealous fellow, to be sure! But do not agitate yourself; be calm, for I have news to impart to you. Yet first let me ask you a question. You aver that you love me better than your own life; that you would die at any time, if it would gain me even a moment's happiness, or a moment's freedom from the cares of life. Now, on your honor, is that true?"

"To be sure it is!" rejoined Surratt. "But why do you ask such a question at such a time, and in such a manner?"

"Well, never mind just yet, my love," said Louise, "until you have answered another query. Suppose it should happen that I accidentally divulged your identity, that I by some fortunate chance should receive a hundred thousand francs, or about twenty-five thousand American dollars for doing so—"

"Miserable creature, I see all now—you have betrayed me! I ought to have known better than to trust my secret with you. Oh, Louise! I who have loved you so madly—I who have given you nearly every centime that I had—to be sold, to be delivered up by you! Great heavens, I shall go mad! Oh, what a punishment! Mother, mother! why did I not, like a man, hasten to your side in the prison cell, and on the scaffold? Why am I not now lying beside you in the grave? What a coward, what a wretch I am! But, Louise Le Grand!" cried Surratt, turning fiercely upon his mistress, "though even now the police may, at your bidding, be just without that door, ready to seize me, they shall never take me alive, neither shall you survive your treachery, to enjoy the money you would coin out of my blood!"

Thus speaking, Surratt whipped out a dagger, and with the bound of a wild beast, sprang at Louise, whom he clutched and drove down upon her knees.

"One minute to pray, and then you die!" hoarsely said Surratt, raising his weapon and glancing at the door of the room

A deadly pallor overspread the cheek of Louise; and gasping for breath, she exclaimed:

"Oh, Jean, Jean! don't. One moment. I would save you, not betray you! Oh, Jean!"

She could say no more; and, sinking still further down, she lay at Surratt's feet in a swoon.

He hastily put away his dagger, and raising the inanimate form, he placed it upon a lounge. Then he ran to a table, got a salts bottle and some water; and in a moment more was kneeling beside Louise, using every effort in his power to recover her. Presently he succeeded, and she opened her eyes. As they fell on him, Louise shuddered.

Surratt called her by all the endearing names he could command, and wept bitterly. Louise, after another interval, fully recovered, and with the aid of her lover, sat up.

"Oh, Jean!" said she, in a weak, faint tone, managing at the same time to twine her finely rounded arm about his neck, "you would have murdered me while saving you. What hour is it?"

As she asked this, a deep anxiety seemed to seize her.

"Half after twelve," answered Surratt, consulting his watch. "Take a sip of this wine, Louise," continued he, reaching a glass which he had filled, "it will strengthen you."

She did so, and then inquired: "Jean, did you ever know a Frenchman named Saint Marie, in America?"

Surratt started as though he had been struck by a bullet, and when he could control himself, replied:

"Great God! Yes, I knew him. But what of him? What did he ask you? What did he tell you? Is he here in Paris, Louise?"

"Shall I tell you all, Jean?" asked Louise, looking strangely at Surratt.

"Yes, yes! for Heaven's sake, tell me all, every jot; for Saint Marie is no friend of mine!"

Louise was well enough by this time to laugh; and at Surratt's earnest exclamations, she did laugh—but only for an instant—and then she replied:

"Well, Jean, my love, I *will* tell you all. As I was leaving the Champs Elysees this morning, I was accosted by a little, insignificant fellow, who beckoned my driver to stop. Said he:

"'Mademoiselle Le Grand, I believe?'

"'Yes, said I.

"'You live in the Rue Lafitte?'

"'Yes.'

"'May I come and see you at two o'clock?'

"'For what object?' I inquired, struck with the assured manner of the man, whose appearance made a deep impression on me.

"'That I will tell you then, Mademoiselle. But one thing you can assure yourself of—it will be a great piece of good fortune to you, if I am correct in my conjectures.'

"'But what is your name?' asked I. 'I do not like to make appointments with strangers.'

"'My name is Lefevre, at your service, Mademoiselle.'

"'Well,' said I, 'you have so greatly awakened my curiosity that I will see you, as you have requested, at two o'clock."

"'Thanks, thanks! Mademoiselle,' answered he, with a low bow; and, raising his hat, he was gone down one of the alleys in a moment.

"Punctually at two o'clock, Lefevre, as he called himself, handed his card to Baptiste, at the lodge, and a minute or so later, was in my presence.

"'Mademoiselle,' he said, opening his business, even before he had deposited his hat and gloves on the table, 'I believe your companion at present is a young English gentleman who is known by the name of Harvey?'

"He waited until I made some answer to this, and I only said, 'Well?' Then he went on, making himself quite at his ease.

"'How long have you known Monsieur Harvey?' he asked.

"'Well, Mr. Lefevre,' I replied, 'it seems to me that you are asking extremely personal questions, and I must have some good reason for answering any of them, before I do so.'

"'Mademoiselle,' rejoined he, 'by answering my questions, you will not only be furthering the ends of justice, but also your own interest—if I am right, and I am certain I am—to the extent of at least twenty-five thousand franks.'

"When he said this, it struck me that he knew, or at least had strong suspicions of who you were, and I resolved on the instant to lead him to suppose that he could make a tool of me. Accordingly I rejoined that, for such a sum as he mentioned, I should be highly delighted to gain any information for him that I could; in fact, assist him in every detail. He thought he had succeeded, and he laid open to me his suspicions and designs. I drew out of him that his real name was Saint Marie; that he had first become acquainted with John H. Surratt in Washington, United States, by meeting him at the house of a Miss Mortimer, to whom both were paying their attentions. Of course it was impossible for two men to be friendly under such circumstances; and the natural distrust and ill-feeling aroused in the breast of Saint Marie was intensified to a fearful degree by the fact that Miss Mortimer expressed to him her desire that he should discontinue his visits to her, as they were distasteful to her friend, Mr. Surratt.

"From that instant Saint Marie determined to be revenged on his successful rival. Necessity drove him to enlist in the Federal army; but here, accidentally, he enjoyed a better opportunity of observing Surratt than he would otherwise have had.

"When he was discharged from the army, he continued to watch Surratt, and finally succeeded in obtaining a situation in the United States detective force, which gave him still more favorable opportunities for securing his object. But Surratt displayed the most extraordinary ability in concealing his trail, and escaping detection at the very moment, too, that it seemed to threaten most certainly. This was in the dispatch and blockade running business.

"Of the assassination plot, Saint Marie learned nothing until after the death of the American President. Then, however, he resumed his vigilance in pursuing Surratt; and from his previous knowledge, he was enabled to get upon his track, and follow him to Montreal, Canada. But there he was so constantly surrounded by his friends, that he could not come near him. Yet he managed to learn that Surratt intended to go to Europe, and he was highly elated at the idea that he would have the longed-for chance of arresting him as he should be getting aboard the steamer. Like the dog in the fable, however, at the same time that he desired revenge, he was greedy for the reward; and he kept his knowledge to himself, in order that he might have the sole honor and sole reward for the arrest. He at once set out for New York, where he arrived, and awaited the coming of Surratt.

"Just at this promising juncture, however, Saint Marie was taken dangerously ill with cholera, by which he was confined to the house for over two weeks. When he recovered sufficiently to go out, he directed his steps to the office of the line of steamers by which he knew Surratt was to have sailed, and, sure enough, he found that his intended prey had escaped under the name of McCarthy, and was by this time in Liverpool, or close there.

"His rage and disappointment scarcely knew any bounds, and he immediately determined to follow Surratt to Liverpool. He did so, and arriving in Liverpool, went to United States Consul Wilding, and made known to him his mission. From him he received money to aid him in his pursuit; and with the addition of some information that Mr. Wilding happened to possess, he soon ascertained that the fugitive had fled from Liverpool to London.

"Thither Saint Marie pursued his man, but got no clue of him until he answered the advertisement of an old, invalid gentleman, who desired the services of a young man to wait upon him."

Until this moment Surratt had listened to Louise's narrative without uttering a single word; but as she reached this point he started, and exclaimed :

"My God! Surely, was that villain, Hendrickson, Saint Marie disguised ?'

Louise resumed :

"He did not say what name he took; but he did say that he was careful to disguise himself before he went to apply for the situation, as something impressed him that the invalid was none other than John H. Surratt. He obtained the preference over all the other applicants, and entered the service of the advertiser. Though he watched him narrowly, he never recognised him; yet at the same time he did discover that his employer was in disguise. Having a friend in the London detective force, Saint Marie, hoping to make some money, informed him concerning the old gentleman, and asked his advice—proposing also, at the same time, to share the proceeds, if there should be any, for arresting him.

"On his return from a visit to this officer, Saint Marie found that his master had, during his absence, disappeared, leaving two trunks, with some contents, and his white wig. On inquiring of the landlady whether she had seen the old man go out, Saint Marie was told :

Not an instant did the desperate fugitive pause, but, uttering a wild yell of defiance, he flung himself headlong over the precipice.

(32)

"'No, he 'ad not gone out; but a 'orrid bad lookin' young man 'ad coom hinto 'is room, and left the 'ouse ; and 'e 'ad the haudacity hactually to wink at 'er.'

"Saint Marie said he felt certain now that his employer was no other than Surratt himself; and he inquired immediately as to his dress and appearance. But the landlady had been so taken up with his *haudacity*, that she had failed to more than casually notice his dress, which, however, she informed Saint Marie, was 'a good deal swellish.'.

"Chagrined, and once more thrown off the track, most any pursuer would have given up the chase. But Surratt's foe was too deadly in his hatred to do so, and he never for a moment relinquished his designs.

"Time rolled on ; and even Saint Marie acknowledges that he began to despair, when suddenly the thought struck him, that the fugitive had left London, and gone to the Continent.

"So away he posted to the passport office, where he ascertained that a young man, answering the meagre description given him by the landlady, had obtained a passport to Paris. Here was a clue, and accordingly to Paris St. Marie went.

"He rightly judged that Surratt would not be long in Paris before he sought the society of kindred spirits. Consequently he loitered about the haunts of the Southern Club, where he ascertained that Surratt was living in the Rue Lafitte with a lady named Louise Le Grand. Hitherto he had experienced such ill-fortune in pursuing his intended victim by himself, that now he resolved to enlist Louise, if possible, to help him. This he thought could be easily done, by the promise of a large reward.

"As I have already told you, I drew all this out of him by pretending to join in his scheme. He said he felt sure you were Surratt, and not Harvey; but this point of identity would have to be settled in presence of witnesses, before he could procure the necessary warrant."

"Well ?" said Surratt, as Louise paused in her narrative.

"He is to be here at one o'clock, with a friend, to see me again—I, in the meantime, to get you into conversation, to find out if you are really Surratt; and then, when he comes here, I was to ask you to step into the reception-room, and in their presence denounce you by name. This done, they will call a gen d'arme, and take you prisoner."

"One o'clock !" exclaimed Surratt, snatching out his watch, and glancing at its dial. "One o'clock ! Why, it wants but five minutes to it now."

"Be calm, my love, be calm," said Louise, "I will never betray you ; and I am sorry I joked you so badly, and thereby placed my life in danger at your hands."

At this instant Baptiste announced Saint Marie, using, however, his assumed name ; for no one knew him properly, save Louise.

A deadly pallor overspread Surratt's features, and he grasped the butt of a revolver beneath his vest, but did not draw it.

2

"Baptiste," said Louise to the servant, "tell him that I will attend him immediately." Then turning to Surratt as Baptiste left the room, she resumed : " Come, Jean, you shall listen outside the door and hear how nicely I will thwart your friend, Saint Marie."

Both then went down, but while Louise entered the apartment in which Saint Marie set awaiting her, with two companions, Surratt remained just outside the half open door, where he was able not only to hear all that was said, but also to see the faces of the three visitors.

The business of the visit was at once broached by the strangers, and, after some half an hour's conversation it was agreed between them and Louise, that she should meet them next morning at eleven o'clock, and go with them before a magistrate and make the necessary affidavits. Saint Marie, in bidding her good night, was extremely pleasant.

ANOTHER FLIGHT.

SURRATT is a person whose disposition is a strange mixture of suspicion and carelessness. This accounts for his partial confessions from time to time, his sudden flights, his cowardice and exceptional acts which seem brave or daring, such, for instance, as leaping over the precipice after his arrest by Cardinal Antonelli.

The morning after the interview, already narrated, occurred between Saint Marie and Louise Le Grand, Surratt determined not to risk remaining until a third interview should take place. He, therefore, told Louise that he intended to return at once to London, but said he must go alone. He promised her to write as soon as he should find a safe retreat there. To this she agreed, and after a mutual exchange of assurances of eternal love and fidelity, the two parted never again to meet.

Instead of doing as he said he would, Surratt went directly to the office of the Paris and Marseilles Road and took passage for the latter city. This was in pursuance of a sudden resolve he had made for fear Louise Le Grand, notwithstanding all her asseverations, intended to betray him. He had determined to fly to Italy and take service in the army of the Pope, as affording him a perfectly safe asylum from pursuit. It will be remembered that the Surratt family were Catholics ; and it has been asserted that in his continual flights, and even immediately after the assassination of President Lincoln, John Surratt was aided and concealed by priests and in monasteries. Such may have been actually true ; but that it was done knowingly we do not for a moment believe ; for though the United States have no treaties whatever with the Papal government, Cardinal Antonelli most promptly had the zouave Watson (Surratt's assumed name) arrested on the mere request of the U. S. consul at Rome.

When Surratt left his apartments, a man in the dress of a French laborer darted out from a deep doorway on the opposite side of the street. This was Saint Marie, who, thus disguised, had resolved, instead of trusting to Louise Le Grande, to watch his prey himself. Stealthily but unflaggingly did the vengeful Canadian dog the steps of Surratt, and he succeeded in finding out the intentions of the fugitive within a few minutes after the latter had taken his passage. The train was to start in two hours, and Surratt loitered about until it was ready. So did Saint Marie, always being careful not to attract Surratt's attention. The pursuer had learned to be far more cautious than previously, and in consequence he was enabled to keep the conspirator constantly under his eye.

Both reached the city of Rome in the same conveyance, and the first thing Surratt did was to go to the recruiting office of the Papal army and enlist as a private in the battalion of zouaves in whose ranks he was afterwards arrested. This act at first dumbfounded Saint Marie, and he thought himself cheated, after all, out of his revenge. But he quickly determined upon enlisting in the same company, and thus he thought he could, after a time, secure his object and have Surratt or Watson, as the fugitive called himself, captured. So, within a few hours, pursuer and pursued were marched together to the barracks near Veroli.

From here Saint Marie wrote to U. S. Minister King at Rome the letter which will be found in the official correspondence further on, and asked that Surratt might be taken. Mr. King at once resolved upon the necessary measures which, as will be remembered, proved successful. Cardinal Antonelli, the Pope's Prime Minister, on the representations made by Mr. King, instantly telegraphed General Kausler, commanding the troops, to have Surratt arrested. This despatch was in turn sent to Lieut. Colonel Allet, Surratt's immediate officer, who as promptly detailed a guard to execute the orders of the Cardinal, and within half an hour Saint Marie saw the completion of his desire, and could not contain himself for joy as the captive was marched out of the barrack building in the midst of six armed soldiers.

"Ha! ha! ha!" he triumphantly laughed, "I am Saint Marie, whom you made your foe. It is my turn now."

Surratt gave him one glance, recognized him, and instantly a paleness overspread his features, while he bit his lips with chagrin to thus find himself in the power of his once despised rival.

"You won't enjoy your triumph long," muttered Surratt to himself, as, turning down the road, he came in sight of the precipice on the edge of which the barracks stood. He had formed the desperate resolve of leaping over this and making his escape through the densely wooded valley below. On tramped the guard with their prisoner, and presently reached the eminence. Now was Surratt's moment. He gathered all his energies, suddenly knocked down the soldier between him and the top of the cliff and bounded away.   His foot was on the edge of the terrible abyss more than a hundred feet deep.   Not an instant did he pause, but with a defiant yell plunged headlong over into the space below, leaving the soldiers too much astounded to move

Almost forty feet down the face of the precipice stood out a ledge or bank on which all the filth of the barrack privies ran, and in this the desperate fugitive fell and thence rolled into the ravine.   Had he leaped a little further he would, beyond doubt, have been dashed to atoms.   The guard gave the alarm and fifty zouaves were soon in pursuit, scouring the valley in all directions.   But their efforts were useless ; and Lieut. Colonel Allet was obliged to telegraph the fact of Surratt's escape across the boundary into Italian territory to Cardinal Antonelli, and the Cardinal in turn to Mr. King.   The latter at once telegraphed Mr. Marsh, U. S. Consul at Florence, and asked him to take up the chase, which that gentleman instantly did, telegraphing to Naples and every other seaport to stop the fugitive from embarking and getting to sea.   This would have been successful but for the following event.   When Surratt, after his fearful leap, was making his way through the almost impenetrable woods which filled the ravine into which he had thrown himself, he chanced upon several ill-looking men, who, from their dress and appearance, he knew were brigands.

Instead of seeking to avoid them, the fugitive, who could scarcely walk from the injuries received in his fall, went to them and telling them that he was a fugitive from justice—though for what he did not say—offered them some money, and offered also to join their band if they would aid him to escape from Naples in some vessel bound to Malta, from whence he could possibly re-embark for Alexandria, Egypt, in which far distant country he felt certain of remaining safe.   The brigands readily agreed to this, and took Surratt with them to one of their hiding places in the mountains. Here he was duly installed with their peculiar ceremonies, and thereby became a member of the band.   As these bands of outlaws infest every section of Italy, and have their spies and members in every village, it was an easy matter to pass their new brother with impunity to Naples.   Here they found that Mr. Marsh was on the watch for the fugitive.   This they however prepared for.   Concealing Surratt in the house of one of their number, another traveled ten miles out of the city to see the captain of a smuggling felucca, in order to get him to take Surratt in his vessel, and after he put to sea to lie in the course of ships to Malta.   Once out thus, there would be no difficulty in placing the conspirator aboard.   Surratt felt now at perfect ease, for he never dreamed that Mr. Marsh would telegraph even to Malta, let alone Alexandria.   Neither did he have any further dread of Saint Marie, the Canadian, for it would be impossible, he argued, that by any event, his vengeful pursuer could get away from the barracks at Veroli.

The brigand who went to see the smuggler, returned at midnight of the day he left Naples, with the intelligence that in two days his felucca, the Falcona, would set sail, and that he would take pleasure in aiding the new brother to escape from the heavy hand of the law.

Still, though everything bore a smiling appearance, the brigands did not neglect to watch every movement of the United States consul, Mr. Marsh, and his active agents. The consequence was, they learned that he had placed twenty men at every avenue, who were to seize Surratt on sight. Not only this, but others were placed along the shore to watch for boats leaving irregularly.

Nothing daunted, however, Surratt's new-found friends resolved to place him aboard the felucca, even if the attempt should result in a conflict. The night selected arrived, and with no little anxiety the fugitive made ready for his further flight. At first it had been arranged that the boat should come from the smuggler's craft after the moon had gone down, and thus give the adventurers the security of darkness. But upon further consideration and consultation, it was resolved that the effort should be made while the moon was up, as Mr. Marsh and his watchers would most likely argue that it would not be made until dark.

Muffled in a large mantle, which, with the help of a broad-rimmed, soft hat, completely concealed his features, Surratt left his hiding place, and stealthily followed a brigand, a good space being between them, down to the beach. Behind him, also at a little distance, walked two more of the brigands, armed to the teeth, and ready, on the slightest alarm, to spring upon any who might interfere with their project.

All went smoothly, and the party reached the spot where it had been previously arranged that the boat which was to carry Surratt should come. In the offing, among several vessels, the felucca was distinctly visible in the brilliant moonlight. The signal that was to bring the boat was made, viz., the shining of two gleams from a bull's-eye lantern having a red glass. And within half a minute after, the party beheld a skiff pushed away from the felucca's side, pulled by a single oarsman.

"Now then is the danger," said the brigands to each other; and all drew their weapons, expecting each instant to be hailed by some concealed officers of Mr. Marsh.

No disturbance occurred, however, and Surratt took his seat safely in the boat, the moment her keel grated on the beach. No time was wasted, as may be supposed, in adieus between the conspirator and his friends, and he was soon safe aboard the felucca. Sail was at once made, and Surratt felt, or rather fancied, himself secure from the vengeful pursuit of Saint Marie.

To show how closely the chase had been kept up by Consul Marsh's men—the brigands had not gone a great distance, on their return toward the city, after the departure of Surratt, before they met a party of three men all of whom they knew immediately were foreigners.

These men eyed them very sharply as they passed by; and when they had gone about twenty yards, they turned and called after the brigands :

"Hallo," said they, "where have you been ?"

"Just down the road a little piece," replied the spokesman of the robbers.

" Whereabouts down the road ?"

As this question was put, the strangers walked back somewhat rapidly in the direction of Surratt's friends, who immediately prepared for a combat, as they felt sure that they would be themselves attacked.

In a few moments the two parties were confronting each other, separated by not more than a few feet.

He who appeared to be the leader of the three who had come from the city, said :

" You say you have been down the road a little piece.   Now, what were you down there for ?"

" Oh," was the prompt reply, "we just went to join a serenading party."

" Why, you have no instruments with you, and this is not the usual hour for serenading."

" We know that, but we left our instruments at Burletti's cafe ; and, beside, we did not intend to go *now* to the serenade."

" Well, did you see a boat put off from shore to a vessel in the bay ?"

" It is possible," was the cautious answer; " but, by all the saints, we swear we did not take particular notice of one.   But why do you ask all this ?"

" Oh, never mind that. "

The three then conversed among themselves in undertones, in English, which one of the brigands slightly understood ; and then turning again, they left the robbers, bidding them a good night.

The brigands were glad to get off so easily; and when they had reached a safe distance, the one who understood English told his companions that the men they had just encountered were emissaries of Consul Marsh, and while talking among themselves, had spoken about the fugitive, and also of arresting the three brigands.

Soon after the robbers were safely ensconsed in a place of refuge, where to arrest them would have been an impossibility, while in the meantime Surratt was going out to sea.   But, as will be seen from the following official correspondence, he had his match in Mr. Marsh.

HONORABLE CHARLES HALE,

United States Consul at Alexandria, Egypt, who finally arrested the fugitive, John H. Surratt, and delivered him into the custody of Admiral Goldsborough.

COMPLETE OFFICIAL DOCUMENTS AND LETTERS CON-
CERNING JOHN H. SURRATT, THE CONSPIRATOR,
SENT TO CONGRESS BY PRESIDENT JOHNSON

To the House of Representatives:

I have the honor to communicate a report of the Secretary of State,
relating to the discovery and arrest of John H. Surratt.

ANDREW JOHNSON.

Washington, December 8, 1866.

Mr. Wilding to Mr. Seward.

[No. 538.]   United States Consulate, Liverpool, Sept. 27, 1865.

Sir—Yesterday, information was given me that ——. Surratt, one of the
persons implicated in the conspiracy to murder Mr. Lincoln, was in Liverpool, or expected there within a day or two. I took the affidavit of the
person who gave me the information, and transmitted it to Mr. Adams;
and I herewith transmit a copy.

—— described himself as a passenger, but I have ascertained that he
is * * *. He expects a letter or visit from Surratt in a day or two, and
has promised to acquaint me with his (Surratt's) location.

Should there be really anything in it, and a warrant be obtained for Surratt's apprehension, we should scarcely get him delivered up without other
evidence than we can obtain here; we should have to ask his remand until
you could send us the necessary evidence.

Very respectfully, I am, sir, your obedient servant,

A. WILDING, *Vice-Consul.*

Hon. William H. Seward.

I, ——, of Montreal, at present residing at ——, make oath and say,
that on the 15th day of this present month of September, on board the
steamer Montreal, sailing from Montreal to Quebec, I became acquainted
with a man passing by the name of Macarthy, a fellow passenger in said
steamer; that on the 16th of said month said Macarthy and I embarked as
passengers on board the steamer ——, for Liverpool, where we arrived
yesterday, the 25th day of September; that said Macarthy was introduced
to me by a Mr. ——, on board the Montreal, as a passenger who had compromised himself; that during the voyage, two or three days after we sailed
from Quebec, during a conversation, said Macarthy spoke of his having had
great difficulty in escaping from the United States into Canada, and asked
me if I suspected who he was. I told him that, connecting what he had
been telling me with what had occurred at the time, I supposed that he had
been connected with the assassination of President Lincoln. He made no
reply, but smiled.

Subsequently, during the voyage, he told me that he had been in the Confederate service, engaged in conveying intelligence between Washington

and Richmond; that he had been concerned in a plan for carrying off President Lincoln from Washington, which was concocted entirely by J. Wilkes Booth and himself; that he came to Canada just before the assassination of President Lincoln took place; that while in Canada he received a letter from Booth, saying that it had become necessary to change their plans, and requested him to come to Washington immediately; that he did start immediately for Washington, but did not say whether he went there; but he said that on his way back to Canada, the train he was in was delayed at St. Albans, and while sitting at breakfast a gentleman next to him spoke of the report of the assassination, and that he, Macarthy, or as he then called himself, Harrison, replied that the news was too good to be true; that the gentleman took a newspaper out of his pocket and read the account of the occurrence, and he, Macarthy, was surprised to see his name there, and left immediately; that on Sunday evening last he had been telling me of an interview with Mr. ——, at Richmond, and I said to him, "You have told me a great deal, what must I call you; what is your real name?" and he said, "My name is Surratt." That was just before our arrival at Londonderry, where he, Macarthy, or Surratt, landed. I have not seen him since, but from what he told me, I believe he is now in Liverpool. He is a man about twenty-five or thirty years of age. As he is now, he is dark; but his hair is dyed. He is about five feet eight inches high; a very sharp Roman nose and prominent forehead, small sunken eyes, slight moustache, no whiskers.   —— ——.

Sworn before me, at Liverpool, this 26th day of September, 1865.

GEORGE MELLY,
Justice of the Peace for the Borough of Liverpool.

Mr. Wilding to Mr. Seward.

[No. 529.]   UNITED STATES CONSULATE, Liverpool, Sept. 30, 1865.

Sir—Since my despatch No. 538, the supposed Surratt has arrived in Liverpool, and is now staying at the oratory of the Roman Catholic church of the Holy Cross. His appearance indicates him to be about twenty-one years of age, rather tall, and tolerably good looking.

According to the reports, Mrs. Surratt was a very devout Roman Catholic; and I know that clergymen of that persuasion, on their way to and from America, have frequently lodged, while in Liverpool, at that same oratory, so that the fact of this young man going there somewhat favors the belief that he is really Surratt.

I can, of course, do nothing further in the matter, without Mr. Adams' instructions and a warrant. If it be Surratt, such a wretch ought not to escape.   *   *   *   *

Very respectfully, I am, sir, your obedient servant,

H. WILDING.

Hon. WILLIAM H. SEWARD, *Secretary of State.*

Mr. Wilding to Mr. Seward.

[No. 544.]   UNITED STATES CONSULATE, Liverpool, Oct. 10, 1865.

Sir—Mr. Adams instructed me that he did not consider it advisable, with our present evidence of identity and complicity, to apply for a warrant for the arrest of the supposed Surratt. In his conversation with the —— of the ——, Surratt declared his hope that he would "live long enough to give a good account of Mr. Johnson."

Very respectfully, I am, sir, your obedient servant,

H. WILDING.

Hon. WILLIAM H. SEWARD, *Secretary of State.*

Mr. Hunter to Mr. Wilding.

[No. 476.] DEPARTMENT OF STATE, Washington, Oct. 13, 1865.

Sir—Your despatches from 533 to 541 inclusive, have been received. In reply to your No. 538, I have to inform you that, upon a consultation with the Secretary of War and the Judge Advocate General, it is thought advisable that no action be taken in regard to the arrest of the supposed John H. Surratt at present. I am, sir, your obedient servant,

W. HUNTER, *Acting Secretary.*

H. WILDING, Esq., *U. S. Vice-Consul, Liverpool.*

Mr. Potter to Mr. Seward.

[No. 236.] UNITED STATES CONSULATE, Montreal, Oct. 25, 1865.

Sir—I sent a telegram in cipher yesterday, informing the department that John H. Surratt left Three Rivers some time in September, for Liverpool, where he is now awaiting the arrival of the steamer Nova Scotian, which sails on Saturday next, by which he expects to receive money from parties in this city, by the hand of ——, of whom Surratt made a confidant in Liverpool. I have the information from ——.

It is Surratt's intention to go to Rome. He was secreted at Three Rivers by a Catholic priest there, with whom he lived.

I requested instructions in my telegram; but hearing nothing yet, I scarcely know what course to take. If an officer could proceed to England in this ship, I have no doubt but that Surratt's arrest might be effected, and thus the last of the conspirators against the lives of the President and Secretary of State be brought to justice. If I hear nothing from Washington, I shall go to Quebec to-morrow to see —— further on the subject.

I have the honor to be, very respectfully, your obedient servant,

JOHN F. POTTER, *United States Consul.*

Hon. WILLIAM H. SEWARD, *Secretary of State.*

Mr. Potter to Mr. Seward.

[No. 237.] UNITED STATES CONSULATE, Montreal, Oct. 27, 1865.

Sir—I have just had a personal interview with ——. He informs me that, before the steamer sailed, a person with whom he was acquainted asked him if he was willing that a gentleman, who had been somewhat compromised by the recent troubles in the United States, should pass as his friend on board the steamer, on her passage out. He declined to acknowledge the person as his friend, until he should know who he was. Subsequently the same party, accompanied by a person, came on board the ship before she left her dock, and introduced him to the surgeon as Mr. McCarty. During the voyage McCarty made himself known to —— as John H. Surratt, and related to him many of the particulars of the conspiracy. He said he had b.een secreted in Montreal most of the time, with the exception of a few weeks, when he was with a Catholic priest, down the river.

He also stated that Porterfield, of this city, formerly of Tennessee, assisted in secreting him.

The —— also informed me that Surratt had dyed his hair, eyebrows and moustache black, stained his face, and wore glasses. Surratt landed at Londonderry, in Ireland, fearing that he might be watched and detected in Liverpool. The —— saw him in Liverpool before the steamer left, when Surratt told him he was obliged to remain until he could receive money from Montreal; and he desired —— to see his friend in this city and bring him funds.

After the return of the Peruvian, —— was transferred to the Nova Scotian. When I saw ——, he had just had an interview with the friend of Surratt, who had introduced him as McCarty, who told him that he was expecting funds from Washington, but that they had not yet come; that he had received letters from Surratt recently, and that he would await in Liverpool the arrival of the Nova Scotian.

I hoped than an officer might have been sent out in the Nova Scotian, which sails to-morrow, in which case —— would have aided him in the arrest of Surratt. The —— says that Surratt manifested no signs of penitence, but justified his action; and was bold and defiant when speaking of the assassination. As an illustration, he told me that Surratt remarked repeatedly, that he only desired to live two years longer, in which time he would serve President Johnson as Booth did Mr. Lincoln. —— said that he felt it his duty to give me this information, for he regarded Surratt as a desperate wretch, and an enemy to society, who should be apprehended and brought to justice. The —— is and ever has been friendly to our government; and I am informed by the most respectable parties, that he is a high-minded, honorable gentleman.

I have the honor to be, very respectfully, your obedient servant,

JOHN F. POTTER, *U. S. Consul.*

Hon. W. H. SEWARD, *Secretary of State.*

Mr. F. W. Seward to Mr. Potter.

[No. 164.]   DEPARTMENT OF STATE, Washington, Nov. 11, 1865.

Sir—Your despatches, from No. 235 to 241, have been received. The information communicated in No. 237 has been properly availed of. * * *

I am, sir, your obedient servant,

F. W. SEWARD, *Assistant Secretary.*

JOHN F. POTTER, Esq., *U. S. Consul.*

Mr. Seward to Mr. Speed.

November 13, 1865.

Sir—I have the honor to transmit herewith for your perusal, despatch No. 237, from John F. Potter, Esq., the United States consul general at Montreal, relative to an interview with —— in relation to John H. Surratt, the conspirator.

In this connection I beg leave to request that you will procure an indictment against the said John H. Surratt as soon as convenient, with the view to demand his surrender.

I will thank you to return the despatch after making such use of it as you may desire.

I have the honor to be, sir, your obedient servant,
WILLIAM H. SEWARD.

Hon. JAMES SPEED, *Attorney General of the United States.*

Mr. King to Mr. Seward.

[No. 53.] LEGATION OF THE UNITED STATES, Rome, April 23, 1866.

Sir—On Saturday last, 21st instant, *   *   *   * called upon me for the purpose, as he said, of communicating the information that John S. Surratt, who was charged with complicity in the murder of President Lincoln, but made his escape at the time from the United States, had recently enlisted in the Papal Zouaves, under the name of John Watson, and was now stationed with his company, the 3d, at Sezze. My informant said that he had known Surratt in America, that he recognized him as soon as he saw him at Sezze; that he called him by his proper name, and that Surratt, taking him aside, admitted that he was right in the guess. He added that Surratt acknowledged his participation in the plot against Mr. Lincoln's life ; and declared that Jefferson Davis had incited, or was privy to it. ———— further, said that Surratt seemed to be well provided with money, and appealed to him ———— not to betray his secret ; and he expressed an earnest desire that if any steps were taken towards reclaiming Surratt as a criminal, he ———— should not be known in the matter. He spoke so positively in answer to my questions as to his acquaintance with Surratt, and the certainty that this was the man ; and there seemed such entire absence of any motive for any false statement on the subject, that I could not very well doubt the truth of what he told me. I deemed it my duty, therefore, to report the circumstance to the department and ask for instructions.

I have the honor to be, with great respect, your obedient servant,
RUFUS KING.

Hon. WILLIAM H. SEWARD, &c.

Mr. King to Mr. Seward.

[No. 54.] LEGATION OF THE UNITED STATES, Rome, May 11, 1866.

Sir—In my last despatch of April 23, I mentioned that ———— had called upon me for the purpose of communicating the intelligence that John S. Surratt, one of the persons charged with complicity in the murder of President Lincoln, was a member of the ———— regiment ———— and then stationed at Sezze I have since received two letters from ———— relating to this matter, which I enclose for the information of the department. While awaiting their instructions, the information has been kept secret here.

I have the honor to be, with great respect, your obedient servant,
RUFUS KING.

Hon. WILLIAM H. SEWARD, *Secretary of State.*

---

* * *, April 23, 1866.

Honorable Sir—With reference to the information I had the honor to give you Saturday last, I most respectfully state and suggest that it would be advisable to proceed at once and ascertain if such information is correct, as I understand that ———— may be soon under orders to go further in the mountains, and it would be more difficult for me to communicate with you. As to the identity of the party, I can assure you, on my most sacred honor, it is lost time to acquire further proofs. I am fully convinced that it is the same individual. I have known him in Baltimore. I have seen him here; have spoken to him; recognized him at once; and when he made himself known to me and acknowledged he was the same party I thought he resembled to. He related several particulars of our first meeting at Ellangowan, fifteen miles from Baltimore, where I was engaged as a teacher, which no one but himself could have remembered. This was about a year before the assassination of President Lincoln; all this occurred about a fortnight ago. I then resolved that as soon as I could get leave to go to Rome, I would seek the American minister and inform him of the fact, which no one here, and I am certain in Europe, knows but myself. I am fully aware of the danger of my position, for in my opinion that party must have friends here, and the utmost caution must be used both in securing him, and for my personal safety. I have told you it is my desire to leave ——— as soon as possible, and that I can do by paying a sum of five or six hundred francs. I think I have done my duty in conscience, and trust in you not to be forgotten. I shall expect an answer at your earliest convenience; in writing to me use ordinary paper and envelope, and take a form and turn of expression as none but myself will be able to understand.

I have the honor to be, honorable sir, very respectfully, your most obedient servant,   ——— ———.

Hon. General KING,

   Minister of the United States, Palazzo Talviata, via Del Corse, Rome.

——————

——, May 7, 1866.

General—I am in receipt of your honored favor of the 4th instant, and in reply beg to state that the party in question is still at the place mentioned in my last letter to you. If any thing happens I shall immediately advise you. Also if I change quarters, I shall let you know where you can address me.

Hoping everything will turn out to your satisfaction and for the greatest advantage of the United States, I hope justice to the ever lamented memory of President L. will be made. I long to revisit my native land and the gray hair of my father and mother, and wish to make the United States my last and permanent home.

I have the honor to be, most respectfully, general, &c.

Hon. General KING, Rome.

——————

Mr. F. W. Seward to Mr Stanton.

DEPARTMENT OF STATE, Washington, May 17, 1866.

Sir—I have the honor to enclose for your information an extract from a despatch to this department of the 23d ultimo, (No. 53,) from Mr. King, minister resident of the United States at Rome, communicating certain information which had been imparted to him by ——— concerning John H. Surratt, who was charged with complicity in the murder of President Lincoln.

I have the honor to be, sir, your obedient servant,

                                         F. W. SEWARD.

Hon. E. M. STANTON, *Secretary of War.*

SURRATT ESCAPING FROM NAPLES AT NIGHT; AIDED BY BRIGANDS, WHOSE BAND HE HAD JOINED.

Mr. Stanton to Mr. Seward.

WAR DEPARTMENT, Washington City, May 19, 1866.

Sir—I have the honor to acknowledge yours of the 17th, accompanying a report of the United States minister at Rome, in relation to John H. Surratt. That report was referred to the Judge Advocate General, who returns it to this department with a recommendation, a copy of which is herewith enclosed. I would respectfully ask that it may be transmitted to Mr. King, with instructions in conformity with General Holt's recommendation. Your obedient servant,

EDWIN M. STANTON.

Hon. F. W. SEWARD, *Acting Secretary of State, &c.*

———

BUREAU OF MILITARY JUSTICE, May 19, 1866.

Respectfully returned, and it is recommended that the American minister at Rome be urged to procure without delay, if possible, a full statement of John H. Surratt's confession to ———, verified by oath, which could probably be obtained through assurances that ——— should in no manner be compromised thereby. This man, there is reason to believe, is the same referred to by one of the witnesses on the trial of the assassins of the President. He was represented to have been engaged in school-teaching in Maryland, at a village called Ellangowan, in the year 1863. Afterwards he came to Washington, and was for a short time employed by ———. He stated that he had come from Montreal, Canada, where he had sold his farm, the proceeds of which he had lost in this country. He spoke French, Italian, and English fluently, and was known as ———. The American minister has no doubt caught the sound of his name imperfectly, and has in consequence written it ———.

The particulars above given will make it easy to ascertain if this is the person mentioned in the despatch to the Secretary of State. If he is, it is believed that it can be shown here that he is a man of character and entitled to credit in his statements It may be added that in this despatch the American minister has slightly mistaken Surratt's name. It is not John S., as he supposes, but John H.

J. HOLT, *Judge Advocate General.*

———

Mr. F. W. Seward to Mr. King.

[No. 35.] DEPARTMENT OF STATE, Washington, May 21, 1866.

Sir—Your despatch of the 23d ultimo, No. 53, was duly received, and a copy of so much of it as relates to John H. Surratt was promptly communicated to the Secretary of War. Enclosed I transmit a copy of a letter from him upon the subject, together with a communication from the Judge Advocate General, to whom your report was referred by the Secretary of War. You are instructed to obtain, if possible, pursuant to General Holt's suggestions, the full statement verified by oath of ———.

I am, sir, your obedient servant,

F. W. SEWARD, *Acting Secretary.*

RUFUS KING, &c., &c., &c., *Rome.*

———

Judge Holt to Mr. F. W. Seward.

BUREAU OF MILITARY JUSTICE, Washington, May 22, 1866.

Dear Sir—Referring to our conversation of this morning, I have the honor to state that the full name of the person supposed to be alluded to in the despatch of the American minister at Rome, is now ascertained to be —— ——. Should he make a statement in regard to Surratt's confession, there should be embodied in it his entire name, together with the circumstances of his sojourn in the United States, if he was here, mentioning dates, places, &c., as well as the names of some of the persons with whom he was associated. This will make the question of identity of easy solution.

Very respectfully, your obedient servant,

J. HOLT, *Judge Advocate General.*

Hon. F. W. SEWARD, *Assistant Secretary of State.*

Mr. F. W. Seward to Mr. King.

[No. 36.]   DEPARTMENT OF STATE, Washington, May 24, 1866.

Sir—Since the date of the instruction addressed to you in answer to your despatch, No. 33, of the 23d ultimo, a letter has been received at this department from Mr. Holt, the Judge Advocate General, in which he states that it has been ascertained that the name of the person supposed to be alluded to in your despatch is ——.

Mr. Holt suggests that if he should make a statement in regard to Surratt's confession, there should be embodied in it his entire name, together with the circumstances of his sojourn in the United States, if he was ever here, mentioning dates, places, &c., as well as the names of some of the persons with whom he was associated. This, Mr. Holt thinks, will make the question of identity one of easy solution.

I am, sir, your obedient servant,

F. W. SEWARD, *Acting Secretary.*

RUFUS KING, Esq., &c., *Rome.*

Mr. Seward to Mr. Wilson.

DEPARTMENT OF STATE, Washington, May 25, 1866.

Sir—I have the honor to acknowledge the receipt of your letter of the 23d instant, asking, on behalf of the Committee on the Judiciary of the House of Representatives, for a copy of all papers in this department which are or may be supposed to implicate any person, other than those already tried, in complicity in the assassination of the late President Lincoln and the attempted assassination of William H. Seward, Secretary of State.

In reply, I have the honor to inform you that there are no papers of that character in this department.

I have the honor to be, sir, your obedient servant,

WILLIAM H. SEWARD.

Hon. JAMES WILSON, *Chairman of the Committee on the Judiciary of House of Representatives.*

Mr. Seward to Mr. Wilson.

[Confidential.]

DEPARTMENT OF STATE, Washington, May 25, 1866.

Sir—In transmitting an official reply to your letter of the 23d instant, it is proper that I should add in this form that we have information from

United States agents in foreign countries in regard to John H. Surratt. It would not now be advisable to communicate this, as the communication might tend to defeat our wish to arrest Surratt for the purpose of bringing him to this country to be tried.

I have the honor to be, sir, your obedient servant,

WILLIAM H. SEWARD.

Hon. JAMES WILSON, *House of Representatives.*

Mr. Seward to Mr. Stanton.

DEPARTMENT OF STATE, May 28, 1866.

Sir—I have the honor to enclose an extract from a despatch received at this department to-day from General King, our minister resident at Rome, in which he communicates further information concerning John H. Surratt. As we have no treaty of extradition with the Papal government, it is proposed that a special agent be sent to Rome to demand the surrender of Surratt, should he be fully identified as the individual referred to by ——, of which there would seem to be but little doubt. I will, consequently, thank you for any suggestions which you may be pleased to offer upon the subject, with a view to such instructions as may be given to the proposed agent. I am, sir, your obedient servant,

WILLIAM H. SEWARD.

Hon. E. M. STANTON, *Secretary of War.*

Mr. King to Mr. Seward.

[No. 56.] LEGATION OF THE UNITED STATES, Rome, June 19, 1866.

Sir—I have the honor to acknowledge receipt of despatch No. 36, under date of May 24, and referring to certain instructions addressed to me, in answer to my despatch No. 53, of the 23d of April. I hasten to say that these instructions have not yet come to hand, and it would appear from the number (36) of the despatch now acknowledged, that two of the series from the State Department, to wit, Nos. 34 and 35, are missing ; the last received previous to the present one being No. 33, of March 23. Under the circumstances, I venture to request that duplicates of Nos. 34 and 35 be at once forwarded to me. Awaiting their arrival, I will act upon the suggestion of the Judge Advocate General referred to in your last, and endeavor to obtain from ——, who is still at Velletri, the further and fuller statement which the Judge deems desirable. —— answers exactly to the description given of him in Judge Holt's letter, and is no doubt the same person. He adheres confidently to his original statement in regard to Surratt, who, at the present speaking, is with —— at Veroli, some forty miles from Rome.

I am, sir, very respectfully, your obedient servant,

RUFUS KING.

Hon. WILLIAM H. SEWARD, *Secretary of State.*

Mr. King to Mr. Seward.

[No. 57.] LEGATION OF UNITED STATES, Rome, June 23, 1866.

Sir—In compliance with the suggestion contained in your last despatch, (No. 36,) I communicated immediately with ——, and received from him yesterday the accompanying document. I had, at the same time, a long conversation with him, which tended to confirm my belief in the truth of his statements. He repeated to me Surratt's confession of complicity in the murder of President Lincoln, and the admission of his mother's guilty participation in the same plot. He said that Surratt was well supplied with money by parties in Paris and London. He avowed his readiness to proceed at once to Washington and testify to all he knew in the premises, only asking to have his expenses paid and some compensation made for his time and trouble. I requested him to describe Surratt to me, which he did; and it corresponded exactly with the description given by the witness Weichmann at the trial of the conspirators. (See page 116 of volume published by Ben. Pittman, recorder, &c.) I cautioned him not to speak of the matter to any one; but to remain quiet until he heard from me, only keeping me advised, from time to time, of his own and Surratt's movements and whereabouts. He returned to Velletri last evening. I await, of course, the receipt of the instructions referred to in despatch No. 36 before taking any further steps in the matter.

I have the honor to be, with great respect, your obedient servant,

RUFUS KING.

Hon. WILLIAM H. SEWARD, *Secretary of State.*

Rome, June 21, 1866.

General—Agreeably with your desire, I have the honor to make the following statement :

1. I am Canadian born, and was living in the United States when the late rebellion broke out. I was engaged as teacher in a small village in Maryland, called Little Texas, or Ellangowan, and there got acquainted with John S. Surratt and William Weichman. About six months before the end of the war I had removed to Washington, and was there engaged in ——. Weichman, who was a friend of Surratt, was there with me. I had occasion to see him several times. He and Weichman, who was the principal witness in the trial of the assassins of President Lincoln, were intimates. From difficulties with Weichman, I left Washington and joined the northern army, as a substitute for E. D. Porter, of Newark, Delaware, principal of an academy in that city. Not being used to hardships, I straggled in the first marches, and was picked up by Stuart's cavalry, near Orange Courthouse, Virginia, and imprisoned in Castle Thunder, Richmond. Having been acquainted with the plots of a company of forgers who were then in the same prison, I acquainted General Winder of their intentions, and as a reward for my services got my liberty, and was sent free to Nassau, and from there to my native home—Canada—having gone first to England, on board a vessel loaded with cotton on the account of the confederacy.

2. After my return home the unfortunate assassination of President Lincoln took place. I immediately went to the United States consul at Montreal, and informed him what I knew about Surratt and Weichman, and told him that in my opinion I thought one was as guilty as the other, and acted only through fear in selling his accomplice. I have met Surratt here in Italy. * * * He has acknowledged to me that he was the instigator of the murder, and had acted in the instructions and orders of persons he did not name, but some of whom are in New York, and others in London. He told me a party in London offered him £10,000 to publish a statement of the affair, but he refused.

I beg to say I am prepared to go to the United States, and give all the evidence I know in the unfortunate matter.

I am personally known in the United States to ——. I have known in Richmond General Winder, Captain Winder, his son; Major Carrington and Major Parkhill, and Captain Alexander, who was then commander of Castle Thunder. I have the honor to be, general, &c.,

—— ——.

General KING, *Rome, Italy.*

Mr. King to Mr. Seward.

ROME, June 30, 1866.

My Dear Governor—As you will learn from the accompanying despatch, the missing document from the State Department arrived all right to-day. I cannot imagine where or how it has been delayed. I will act forthwith upon the instructions in regard to ——. He is willing and anxious to go to the United States, and can get his release by paying fifty dollars or so. I should judge that his parole evidence would be much more desirable than any certified statement. He would expect to have his expenses paid, and some compensation made for his time. Faithfully yours,

RUFUS KING.

Hon. WILLIAM H. SEWARD.

Mr. King to Mr. Seward.

[No. 59.]   LEGATION OF THE UNITED STATES, Rome, July 14, 1866.

Sir—In compliance with instructions heretofore received, I have obtained, and herewith transmit, an additional statement, sworn and subscribed to by ——, touching J. H. Surratt's acknowledged complicity in the assassination of the late President Lincoln. —— again expressed to me his great desire to return to America and give his evidence in person. He thinks that his life would be in danger here, should it be known that he had betrayed Surratt's secret.

I have the honor to be, with great respect, your obedient servant,

RUFUS KING.

Hon. WILLIAM H. SEWARD, *Secretary of State.*

ROME, July 10, 1866.

I, ——, a native of Canada, British America, aged thirty-three, do swear and declare, under oath, that about six months previous to the assassination of President Abraham Lincoln, I was living in Maryland, at a small village called Ellangowan, or Little Texas, about twenty-five or thirty miles from Baltimore, where I was engaged as teacher for a period of about five months. I there and then got acquainted with Lewis J. Weichmann and John H. Surratt, who came to that locality to pay a visit to the parish priest. At that first interview, a great deal was said about the war and slavery—the sentiments expressed by these two individuals being more than strongly secessionists. In the course of the conversation, I remember Surratt to have said that President Lincoln would certainly pay for all the men that were slain during the war. About a month after I removed to Washington, at the instigation of Weichmann, and got a situation as tutor, where he was himself engaged. Surratt visited us weekly, and once he offered to send me south, but I declined. I did not remain more than a month at Washington, not being able to agree with Weichmann, and enlisted in the army of the North, as stated in my first statement in writing to General King.

I have met Surratt here in Italy, at a small town called Velletri. He is now known under the name of John Watson. I recognised him before he made himself known to me, and told him privately, "You are John Surratt, the person I have known in Maryland." He acknowledged he was, and begged of me to keep the thing secret. After some conversation, we spoke of the unfortunate affair of the assassination of President Lincoln, and these were his words: "Damn the Yankees, they have killed my mother; but I have done them as much harm as I could. We have killed Lincoln, the nigger's friend." He then said, speaking of his mother, "Had it not been for me and that coward, Weichmann, my mother would be living yet. It was fear that made him speak. Had he kept his tongue, there was no danger for him; but if I ever return to America, or meet him elsewhere, I shall kill him."

He then said he was in the secret service of the South. And Weichmann, who was in some department there, used to steal copies of the despatches and forward them to him, and thence to Richmond. Speaking of the murder, he said they had acted under the orders of men who are not yet known, some of whom are still in New York, and others in London. I am aware that money is sent to him yet from London. "When I left Canada," he said, "I had but little money, but I had a letter for a party in London. I was in disguise, with dyed hair and false beard. That party sent me to a hotel, where he told me to remain till I would hear from him. After a few weeks he came, and proposed to me to go to Spain, but I declined, and asked to go to Paris. He gave me £70, with a letter of introduction to a party there, who sent me here to Rome, where I joined the Zouaves." He says he can get money in Rome at any time. I believe he is protected by the clergy, and that the murder is the result of a deep laid plot, not only against the life of President Lincoln, but against the existence of the republic—as we are aware that priesthood and royalty are and always have been opposed to liberty. That such men as Surratt, Booth, Weichmann, and others should, of their own accord, plan and execute the infernal plot which resulted in the death of President Lincoln, is impossible. There are others behind the curtain, who have pulled the strings to make these scoundrels act.

I have also asked him if he knew Jefferson Davis; he said no, but that he had acted under the instructions of persons under his immediate orders. Being asked if Jefferson Davis had anything to do with the assassination, he said, "I am not going to tell you." My impression is that he brought the order from Richmond, as he was in the habit of going there weekly. He must have bribed the others to do it; for when the event took place, he told me he was in New York, prepared to fly as soon as the deed was done. He says he does not regret what has taken place, and that he will visit New York in a year or two, as there is a heavy shipping firm there who had much to do with the South; and he is surprised that they have not been suspected.

This is the exact truth of what I know about Surratt. More I could not learn, being afraid to awaken his suspicions. And further I do not say.

———————

Sworn and subscribed before me, at the American Legation at Rome, this 10th day of July, A. D. 1866, as witness my hand and seal of office.

RUFUS KING, *Minister Resident.*

JOHN H. SURRATT.

Surratt, while a fugitive, adopted a great number of various disguises, at times cutting his hair close, at others wearing wigs. Sometimes he wore a beard, and sometimes a moustache and imperial; while his different suits of clothes were almost without number; so that all other pictures of him are not likenesses at all.

JOHN H. SURRATT, THE CONSPIRATOR.   67

Mr. King to Mr. Seward.

ROME, July 14, 1866.

My dear Governor—I send herewith ——'s sworn statement, (as made out by himself,) about Surratt's confession. —— is very anxious to return to America, and give his evidence in person, before the Judge Advocate General. He thinks that his life would be in danger, if it became known that he had betrayed Surratt's secret. He is very desirous, too, to see his old mother, still living in Canada, and in straitened circumstances. It would not be difficult nor expensive to procure his discharge, ship him to Havre, and thence, with the help of the United States Consul there, to New York, always providing that his presence and evidence are wanted in Washington.   Very truly, &c.,

RUFUS KING.

Hon. WILLIAM H. SEWARD.

Mr. Seward to Mr. King.

[No. 40.]   DEPARTMENT OF STATE, Washington, July 16, 1866,

Sir—In further acknowledgment of your despatch of the 23d of June, I have to inform you that I have laid before the Secretary of War the letter which accompanies it, and which was written by —— on the 21st of June last.   I am, sir, your obedient servant,

WILLIAM H. SEWARD.

RUFUS KING, Esq.

Mr. Seward to Mr. Stanton.

DEPARTMENT OF STATE, Washington, July 20, 1866.

Sir—I have just received from Mr. Rufus King, our minister at Rome, a private communication, dated June 30, in which the following sentence occurs concerning ——:

"As you will learn from the accompanying despatch, the missing document from the State Department arrived all right to-day. I cannot imagine where or how it has been delayed. I will act forthwith upon the instructions in regard to ——. He is willing and anxious to go to the United States, and can get his release by paying fifty dollars or so. I should judge that his parole evidence would be more desirable than any certified statement. He would expect to have his expenses paid, and some compensation made for his time."

I send the above extract for your own information and that of the Bureau of Military Justice.   I am, sir, your obedient servant,

WILLIAM H. SEWARD.

Mr. Seward to Mr. Stanton.

DEPARTMENT OF STATE, Washington, Aug. 7, 1866.

Sir—I send you herewith, for your further information, a transcript of a despatch of the 14th of July last, (No. 59,) from the United States minister at Rome, together with a copy of an additional statement, sworn and subscribed to by ——, touching John H. Surratt's acknowledged complicity in the assassination of the late President Lincoln.

I have the honor to be, sir, your obedient servant,

WILLIAM H. SEWARD.

Hon. EDWIN M. STANTON, *Secretary of War.*

Mr. King to Mr. Seward.

[No. 62.]   U. S. LEGATION, Rome, Aug. 8, 1866.

Sir—I availed myself of the opportunity to repeat to the Cardinal the information communicated to me by ——, in regard to John H. Surratt His eminence was greatly interested by it, and intimated that if the American Government desired the surrender of the criminal, there would probably be no difficulty in the way.

I am, sir, very respectfully, your obedient servant,

RUFUS KING.

Hon. WILLIAM H. SEWARD, *Secretary of State.*

———

Mr. Seward to Mr. King.

STATE DEPARTMENT, Washington, Aug. 15, 1866.

Sir—I have to acknowledge the receipt of your despatch of the 14th of July, (No. 59,) and your private note of the same date, and to inform you, in reply, that I have enclosed a copy of the former, together with the sworn statement of ——, which accompanied it, for the consideration of the Secretary of War.   I am, sir, your obedient servant,

WILLIAM H. SEWARD.

RUFUS KING, Esq.

———

Mr. Seward to Mr. King.

No. 43.]   DEPARTMENT OF STATE, Washington, October, 16, 1866.

Sir—Mr. King's private letter of September 12, written at Hamburg, has just been received. It is accompanid by a private letter from——, of the 12th of September —— to Mr. Hooker.

I think it expedient that you do the following things:

1. Employ a confidential person, not ——, to visit Velletri, and ascertain, by comparison with the photograph herewith sent, whether the person indicated by —— is really John Surratt.

2. Pay —— to —— in consideration of the information he has already communicated on the subject.

3. Seek an interview with Cardinal Antonelli, and, referring to an intimation made by him to Mr. King in a conversation which took place on the 7th of August last, as reported in Mr. King's No. 62, namely, "that if the American government desired the surrender of the criminal (Surratt) there would probably be no difficulty in the way," ask the cardinal whether his Holiness would now be willing, in the absence of an extraditon treaty, to deliver John H. Surratt upon authentic indictment and at the request of this department, for complicity in the assassination of the late President Lincoln, or whether, in the event of this request being declined, his Holiness would enter into an extradition treaty with us, which would enable us to reach the surrender of Surratt.

4. Ask as a favor from this government that neither —— nor Surratt be discharged —— until we shall have had time to communicate concerning them after receiving a prompt reply to this communication from you. —— should be told confidentially that the subject of his communication to Mr. Hooker is under consideration here.   I am, sir, your obedient servant,

W. H. SEWARD.

P. S.—The photograph intended to be enclosed with this instruction will be sent by the next mail.

Mr. King to Mr. Seward.

No. 65.]   LEGATION OF THE UNITED STATES AT ROME, November 2, 1866.

Sir—I hasten to acknowledge your despatch No. 43, marked "confidential," under date of October 16, in reply to my private letter of September 12, from Hamburg, and conveying instructions upon the subject therein referred to. I lost no time in seeking an interview with the cardinal secretary of state, as directed to do in the aforesaid despatch; and with that view proceeded this morning to the Vatican, accompanied by Mr. Hooker, acting secretary, as well that he should hear the conversation between the cardinal and myself, as that he should repeat to his Eminence in Italian what I proposed saying to him in French, relative to the wishes and expectations of our government in relation to Surratt. We were fortunate in finding the cardinal alone and disengaged, and I proceeded at once to state the business upon which we had called. His eminence was greatly interested in the matter, the more so as I showed him the portraits of the "conspirators," contained in the volume published by "Ben. Pittman," and entitled "Assassination of President Lincoln"—remembered very well our previous conversation on the same subject, (referred to in my despatch No. 62, of August 8th,) and the intimation he then gave as to the disposition of the Papal authorities to surrender Surratt, should he be claimed by the American government; and in reply to my question whether, upon authentic indictment or the usual preliminary proof, and at the request of the State Department, he would be willing to deliver up John H. Surratt, frankly replied in the affirmative. He added that there was, indeed, no extradition treaty between the two countries, and that to surrender a criminal, where capital punishment was likely to ensue, was not exactly in accordance with the spirit of the Papal government; but that in so grave and exceptional a case, and with the understanding that the United States government, under parallel circumstances, would do as they desired to be done by, he thought the request of the State Department for the surrender of Surratt would be granted. I then requested as a favor to the American government, that neither Surratt nor —— should be discharged from the Papal service until further communication from the State Department, and his Eminence promised to advise with the Minister of War to that effect. I thanked his eminence for his prompt and frank replies to my queries, and assured him that they would give great satisfaction to our government.

I shall, as directed, employ a trusty and confidential person to proceed to the station where Surratt is, and identify him by the photograph which I expect to receive in the next despatch from the department, and I will pay —— the sum named by the Secretary, in consideration of the information already furnished. I may also hold out to him the hope of some further remuneration, should Surratt be identified and surrendered, as also of his speedy discharge, in order to be a witness against Surratt, if required in the United States. Having thus, I trust, satisfactorily fulfilled the wishes of the State Department, I await with interest further instructions on this subject.

I have the honor to be, very respectfully, your obedient servant,

RUFUS KING.

HON. WILLIAM H. SEWARD, *Secretary of State.*

Mr. King to Mr. Seward.—[Private.]

Rome, November 3, 1866.

My Dear Governor—In the accompanying despatch, No. 65, you will find the formal reply to yours of October 16, which I duly received two days ago. Both Mr. Hooker and myself referred, as much from the cardinal's manner as from what he said, that there would be no difficulty about the surrender of Surratt should he be claimed. In this event, how is he to be sent to America? Cannot one of our ships-of-war, now in the Mediterranean, be directed to come to Civita Vecchia, secure Surratt and —— on board, and convey them to the United States? Would it not be well to ask also for —— discharge, that he may be used, if required, as a witness at Surratt's trial? Am I to draw directly on the department, or on Baring Brother, for ——, and the expense of sending a person to Veroli to identify Surratt?

Faithfully,   RUFUS KING.

Mr. King to Mr. Seward.

No. 66.]   LEGATION OF THE UNITED STATES, Rome, November 16, 1866.

Sir—In my despatch No. 65, under date of November 2, I mentioned the result of the interview I had with the cardinal secretary of state on the subject referred to in your "confidential" communication of October 16. I had occasion yesterday to call again upon his Eminence, with the view to ascertain if possible, the truth of the widely prevalent rumor that the Pope intended leaving Rome and seeking a refuge in the island of Malta. Before, however, I had the opportunity of making this inquiry, the cardinal apprised me that John Watson, alias John H. Surratt, had been arrested by his orders, and while on the way to Rome had made his escape from the guard of six men in whose charge he had been placed. At the same time his Eminence handed me the official documents, copies of which I herewith transmit, relating to the arrest, the escape, and the subsequent pursuit. As Veroli is close to the frontier, it is not at all unlikely that Surratt will make good his escape from his Zouave pursuers into the Italian kingdom. I thought it well, therefore, to send a confidential person at once to Florence, to lay the whole case before the American minister, and solicit his aid and that of the Italian government in the recapture; for I did not feel at all sure that either a message by telegraph or a letter by mail, to Mr. Marsh, would, under the circumstances, escape the surveillance or possible interruption of the Papal authorities. I hope to have a report from my messenger within two or three days, and as Surratt was in his Zouave dress when he effected his escape, I think the chance a fair one that he will be retaken. I trust that the course which I have pursued in the premises will meet the approbation of the department. I feel bound to add that, incredible as the details of the story appear, the cardinal spoke of them as verified beyond all question, and expressed very great and apparently sincere regret at Surratt's escape.

I have the honor to be, very respectfully, your obedient servant,

RUFUS KING.

Hon. WILLIAM H. SEWARD, *Secretary of State.*

November 6, 1866.

Colonel—Cause the arrest of the Zouave Watson, and have him conducted, under secure escort, to the military prison at Rome. It is of much importance that this order be executed with exactness.

The general, pro-minister,

KAUZLEI.

Lieut. Colonel ALLET, *Commanding Zouave Battalion, Velletri.*

No. 463.] PONTIFICAL ZOUAVES, BATTALION HEADQUARTERS, Velletri, Nov. 7, 1866.

General—I have the honor to inform you that the Zouave, John Watson, has been arrested at Veroli, and will be taken, to-morrow morning, under good escort, to Rome. While he was searched for at Trisulti, which was his garrison, he was arrested by Captain De Lambilly, at Veroli, where he was on leave. I have the honor also to inform your excellency that his name is not Waston, but Watson.

I have the honor to be, general, your excellency's very humble and obedient servant,

Lieutenant Colonel ALLET,

His Excellency the GENERAL, *Minister of War, Rome.*

[PONTIFICIAL TELGRAPH.—Presented at Valletri, Nov. 8, 1866, at 8.35 A. M. Received at Rome, Nov. 8, 1866, at 8.50 A. M.]

His Excellency, the Minister of War, Rome—I received the following telegram, dated ——, from Captain Lambilly:

"At the moment of leaving the prison, surrounded by six men as guards, Watson plunged into the ravine, more than a hundred feet deep, which defends the prison. Fifty zouaves are in pursuit. I will send Y. E. the news which I shall receive by telegraph.

Lieutenant-Colonel ALLET."

[No. 602.] WAR DEPARTMENT, OFFICE OF THE MINISTER, Nov. 8, 1866.

Your Reverend Eminence—I have the honor to transmit to your very reverend eminence the enclosed documents about the arrest and escape of Zouave Watson, of the third company, and will not fail to transmit the latest news I shall receive of the result of the pursuit of that individual.

I bend in all humility before the sacred Pontiff, with fresh assurances of profound respect.

I am, your eminence, your most humble and devoted servant,

KAUSLEI.

His Eminence, the Cardinal ANTONELLI, *Secretary of State.*

Mr. Harvey to Mr. Seward.

[No. 414.] LEGATION OF UNITED STATES, Lisbon, Nov. 17, 1866.

Sir—I communicate herewith a copy of a telegram which reached me early this morning:

Rome, November 16, 1866—11.50 A. M.

His Excellency Mr. HARVEY, *American Minister, Lisbon:*

Inform Admiral Goldsborough that very important matters render the immediate presence of one of our ships-of-war necessary at Civita Vecchia.

RUFUS KING.

G. V. FOX.

As Rear-Admiral Goldsborough is not now in port, I sent immediately for Commodore Steedman, who arrived here some days ago, and who is now the superior officer present, in order to consult with him as to the proper measures to be adopted.

The United States steamer Swatara left here yesterday for Tangier, Gibraltar, and others ports in the Mediterranean, and if the rear-admiral, who is believed to have quit Cherbourg for Lisbon within the last few days, does not appear as soon as now anticipated, Commodore Steedman will intercept and order the Swatara by telegraph to proceed to Cevita Vecchia.

In the meantime I have addressed the following telegrams to the rear-admiral and to our minister at Rome :

Lisbon, Nov. 17, 1866

Rear-Admiral Goldsborough, *U. S. S. Colorado, Cherbourg:*

Our minister at Rome and Mr. Fox have telegraphed me to request you to send a ship immediately to Cevita Vecchia. Quarantine has been removed from all French ports.

J. E. H.

Lisbon, November, 17, 1866.

General Rufus King, *Ameri<an Minister, Rome* :

Rear-Admiral Goldsborough is expected here daily. If he is delayed, I have arranged to send you ship Swatara.   J. E. H.

These are the only precautions that could be taken under the circumstances, and they are believed to be sufficient for the emergency.

I have the honor to be, sir, your most obedient servant,

JAMES E. HARVEY.

Hon. William H. Seward, *Secretary of State.*

Mr. Marsh to Mr. Seward.

[No. 168.]   Legation of United States, Florence, Nov. 18, 1866.

Sir—On my arrival from Venice on Tuesday morning I found the papers, copies and translations of which, marked respectively A, B, C, D, and E, are hereunto annexed. Mr. Macpherson, introduced by the letter marked A, had gone to Leghorn, and I had no other information on the subject of his mission than such as the papers above referred to furnished.

I lost no time in seeing the secretary general of the ministry of foreign affairs—the minister not having yet returned from Venice—stated to him such facts as I was possessed of, and inquired whether he thought his government would surrender Surratt to the United States for trial if he should be found in the Italian territory.

He replied that he thought the accused would be surrendered on proper demand and proof, but probably only under a stipulation on our part that the punishment of death would not be inflicted on him. Having no instructions on the subject, knowing nothing of those which Mr. King might have received, and having, moreover, at that time no reason to suppose that Surratt had escaped into the territory of the King of Italy, I did not pursue the discussion further.

On Thursday Mr. Macpherson returned, but the information he was able to give me related only to the mode of the detection of Surratt.

On Friday morning, the 16th, I received Mr. King's two letters, copies of which, marked F and G, are annexed, and at 8 P. M. the same day a telegram, of which a copy, marked H, is also attached.

SURRATT'S FINAL ARREST.

"You're John Surratt!" exclaimed Consul Hale, seizing the stranger. "Don't draw that dagger! or I'll shoot you! You are my prisoner! in the name of the United States Government! Ho! there, bring those manacles!

Upon the receipt of the telegram I immediately addressed and sent to the ministry of foreign affairs a note of which I annex a copy, marked I, and I called twice at the foreign office the next (Saturday) morning, but learned that the ministry of grace and justice, to which my note had been referred, had not come to decision on the subject. I presented such additional views as had suggested themselves to me in the mean time, and expressed an earnest hope that the request of my note for the detention of Surratt until more formal proceedings could be had, would be acceded to.

The secretary general of the ministry of foreign affairs, whom I saw in the absence of the minister, appeared to me less favorably disposed to the application than I had expected from my former conversation with him, and at a later hour I addressed to the ministry a note, of which a copy, marked J, is annexed hereto.

I doubt whether, in case of the surrender of Surratt, a formal stipulation to exempt him from the punishment of death will be insisted. In the famous La Gala case, Mr. Visconti Venosta, then as now minister of foreign affairs, refused to enter into such a stipulation on the extradition of the offenders, but nevertheless the government yielded to the intercessions of the Emperor of France, and the sentence of those atrocious criminals, though convicted of numerous murders, robberies, and even cannibalism, was commuted, and I suppose the government of Italy would strongly recommend Surratt to mercy, if he is surrendered to us. The public sentiment of all classes in Italy is decidedly averse to the infliction of capital punishment, and I shall not go too far, if I add to any severe or adequate punishment for the gravest offenses. The universality of this feeling will have its weight with the government.

In order to secure the transmission of this despatch by the next mail, it must be posted at so early an hour to-morrow morning that I shall not be able to see the minister or secretary general of foreign affairs before it is sent to the post office, and I cannot probably communicate the decision of the ministry until another mail.

I have written to ask Mr. King for a copy of so much of his instructions on this subject as may be useful to me, and I beg for special instructions for my own guidance in the further conduct of this affair.

I have the honor to be, sir; your most obedient servant,

GEORGE P. MARSH.

Hon. W. H. SEWARD, *Secretary of State.*

Mr. King to Mr. Marsh.

LEGATION OF UNITED STATES, Rome, November 9, 1866.

My Dear Sir—I send to you, under very peculiar circumstances, and as bearer of despatches, my friend Mr. Robert Macpherson. He will tell you the story which the accompanying despatches will help to illustrate. I need not ask you to aid him in his researches.

Very truly yours, RUFUS KING.

Mr. MARSH, *United States Minister, Florence.*

Kausler to Cardinal Antonelli.

MINISTRY OF ARMS, November 8, 1866.

Most Reverend Eminence—I have the honor to transmit to your most reverend eminence the accompanying documents on the arrest and escape

4

of the Zouave Watson, of the 3d company, and I shall not fail to communicate such further information as I may receive as to the result of the pursuit of the individual.

Bowing to kiss the sacred purple, I am proud to subscribe myself, with profound devotion, yonr most Reverend Eminence's most humble and most devoted servant,

.KAUSLER.

His most Reverend Eminence the CARDINAL ANTONELLI,
Secretary of State.

———

November 6, 1866.

Colonel—Cause the Zouave Watson to be arrested and conveyed under safe escort to the military prisons at Rome. It is of much importance that this order be scrupulonsly fulfilled.

The general pro-minister,   KAUSLER.

Lieutenant-Colonel ALLET,
Commanding the Battalion of Zouaves, Velletri.

———

PONTIFICAL ZOUAVES, Velletri, November 7, 1866.

General—I have the honor to inform yon that the Zouave Watson (John) has been arrested at Veroli, and will be conducted to-morrow morning, under good escort, to Rome.

While they were in search of him at Trisulti, his garrison, he was arrested by Captain de Zambilly at Veroli, where he was on leave.

I have the honor to inform your excellency that his name is not *Waston* but *Watson.*

I have the honor to be, general, your excellency's most humble subordinate,   Lieutenant-Colonel ALLET.

His Excellency the GENERAL, *Minister of Arms, Rome.*

———

[Telegram presented at Velletri, Nov. 8, 1866, 8.35 A. M.; arrived at Rome, Nov. 8, 1866, 8.50 A. M.]

His Excellency the General Minister of Arms, Rome:

I received the following telegram, dated 4.30 A. M., from Captain Zambilly:

At the moment he left the prison, and while surrounded by six men as a guard, Watson threw himself into the ravine, above a hundred feet perpendicular in depth, which defends the prison. Fifty zouaves in pursuit of him.

I will transmit to your excellency the intelligence I may receive by telegraph.   ALLET, *Lieutenant-Colonel.*

———

LEGATION OF THE UNITED STATES, Rome, Nov. 12, 1866.

My dear Mr. Marsh—I send you one of the photographs of John Surratt, which I received this day from the State Department, and may help to identify the scoundrel, if we should be fortunate enough to catch him.

Very truly, yours,
RUFUS KING.

· ROME, November 13.

My dear Mr. Marsh—I had another interview and long conversation with Cardinal Antonelli this morning in reference to the arrest and escape of John H. Surratt. The Cardinal gave me the reports of the various officers charged with the investigation of the facts in the case. They certainly show, on the surface, perfect good faith on the part of the Papal authorities, and an earnest desire to arrest the criminal, of whose guilt the Cardinal expressed himself fully satisfied. He added that Surratt had, beyond doubt, made good his escape into the Italian territory, and was now, doubtless, at Naples.

I write to give you this information, as it may aid your researches. I still think and hope we may catch the fugitive.   Very truly, yours,

RUFUS KING.

——

[Telegram, presented the 15th, 4.30 o'clock; received the 16th, 8.25 o'clock.]

ROME.

Mr. Marsh, American Minister, Florence—I have just heard that Surratt has been admitted, wounded, into the hospital at Sora.

RUFUS KING.

——

LEGATION OF THE UNITED STATES, Florence, Nov. 16, 1866.

Mr. Minister—I am credibly informed, and confidently believe, that John H. Surratt, a leading actor in the assassination of Abraham Lincoln, late President of the United States, who escaped from justice after that event, and has been recently serving as a Zouave in the Papal army at Rome, is now in a hospital at Sora, (supposed Sora terra di Lavoro,) where he is said to have been admitted in consequence of a wound received in some manner, of which I am not informed.

It has been known for a considerable time to the legation of the United States at Rome, that Surratt had enlisted in the Papal military service; and this fact having been communicated by the legation to the Pontificial government, an order for his arrest and committal to the military prison at Rome was issued by the Minister of War on the 6th of the present month.

In pursuance of this order, Surratt, who had enrolled himself by the name of John Watson, was arrested at Veroli on the following day, and conducted to Velletri. On the 8th of the month he escaped from his keepers, and has not been since heard of until his admission to the hospital at Sora.

The circumstances of the assassination in question are so well known, that I need not enter into any details on that subject; and this legation, as well as the government and people of the United States, have received such abundant proof of the intense horror with which this great crime was regarded by the Italian government and nation, that I cannot doubt the entire readiness of the public authorities of this kingdom to use all proper measures to bring to justice any of the participators in the offence who may be found within their jurisdiction.

I am, as may naturally be supposed, without conclusive evidence to prove at this moment the complicity of Surratt in the crime, or to show the identity of that individual and the person now in the hospital at Sora. The latter point, however, I am informed, can be established at once and beyond dispute ; and the printed record of the proceedings against the assassins—a copy of which accompanies this note—will, I doubt not, be considered sufficient *prima facie* evidence of the guilt of the accused to warrant his detention until further proof, if any be necessary, can be produced to justify his extradition to the authorities of the United States for trial.

I need not enlarge upon the heinous criminality and the dangerous character of the offence with which Surratt is charged.   The punishment of the assassins interests all civilized commonwealths, and the cause of justice is, in this instance, the cause of organized government, of public order, and of national security throughout the world.

I pray, therefore, Mr. Minister, that the local authorities at Sora may be instructed to hold the accused in safe custody until further proceedings can be had to insure his surrender to such officers of the United States as shall be authorized to receive him.

I avail myself of this occasion to tender to you, Mr. Minister, the renewed assurances of my high consideration.

GEORGE P. MARSH.

Commander VISCONTI VENOSTA, *Minister of Foreign Affairs.*

Mr. Marsh to Visconti Venosta.

LEGATION OF THE UNITED STATES, Florence, Nov. 17, 1866.

Mr. Minister—I have the honor to enclose herewith a photographic portrait of John H. Surratt, alias Watson, supposed to be now in hospital at Sora.   The portrait was received by the United States legation at Rome from the government of the United States, and is therefore, no doubt, authentic.   It may help to identify the individual at Sora with the accused ; but, as it is not apparently of the most recent date, it is not improbable that time and the circumstances of Surratt's life for the last eighteen months may have produced some change in his features and expression, which will render the likeness between the original and the portrait less striking.   The point of identity, however, as I had the honor of stating to Mr. Cerutti this morning, can, it is believed, be satisfactorily established by the testimony of persons at Rome, who have known Surratt familiarly on both sides of the Atlantic.

Accept, Mr. Minister, the renewed assurance of my high consideration.

GEORGE P. MARSH.

Commander VISCONTI VENOSTA, *Minister of Foreign Affairs.*

Mr. King to Mr. Seward.

[No. 67.]   LEGATION OF THE UNITED STATES, at Rome, Nov. 19, 1866.

Sir—I had hoped ere this to have been able to announce to the department the fact of the recapture of John H. Surratt, whose arrest and subsequent escape were mentioned in my last despatch ; but I regret to say that thus far all our efforts to apprehend the fugitive have proved fruitless. Mr. Marsh, our minister at Florence, will no doubt report to the government the steps which he may have seen fit to take in the premises.   I shall, therefore, content myself with a brief recital of what was done here.

On Friday last, November 16th, General Kacsler, the Papal minister of war, called to inform me of a rumor which had reached him, that Surratt had been received, wounded, into the military hospital at Sora, a few miles beyond the Papal frontier. I instantly telegraphed this information to Mr. Marsh, and in a few hours received a reply from him to the effect that he had made the necessary application to the Italian government. Regarding, however, the identification and apprehension of Surratt as of the first importance, I despatched Mr. Hooker, acting secretary of legation, by the earliest train to Sora, furnished with all the necessary documents and a photograph of Surratt, and also with instructions, if he found Surratt there, to ask, in the name of the American government, that he should be held in close custody until a proper demand could be made upon the Italian authorities for his surrender as a fugitive from justice. Mr. Hooker executed his mission with intelligence and despatch. Arriving at Isoletta, the frontier station, and communicating by telegraph with the commanding officer at Sora, he ascertained that one of the Pontifical Zouaves, calling himself Watson, of Richmond, United States, twenty-two years old, tall, fair complexion, blue eyes, high forehead, reddish (sandy) hair, moustaches and goatee, had passed Sora for Naples, on the 8th instant, the same day that he escaped from Veroli, only a few miles distant. Mr. Hooker at once telegraphed this intelligence to our consul at Naples. The officer in charge at Isoletta did the same to the Neapolitan chief of police. Both asked that Surratt should, if possible, be arrested. I received a prompt reply from Mr. Swan, at Naples, acknowledging the receipt of Mr. Hooker's telegram, and stating that they were on the lookout for Surratt. Our hopes were strong, therefore, that we should succeed in catching him somewhere in the vicinity of Naples. But yesterday a second despatch from Mr. Swan apprised us that Surratt had left the preceding day, November 17th, for Alexandria, by a steamer which stopped at Malta to coal, and that he had telegraphed the facts to our consul at that point. I also immediately telegraphed to Mr. Winthrop, at Malta, urging the arrest of Surratt; but up to the moment of closing this despatch I have received no reply from Mr. Winthrop. The probabilities now are, I fear, that Surratt will make good his escape.

Some surprise perhaps may be expressed that Surratt was arrested by the Papal authorities, before any request to that effect had been made by the American government. This was alluded to in a conversation I had on the subject with Cardinal Antonelli and the Minister of War, on Friday last. Both gave me to understand that the arrest was made with the approval of his Holiness, and in anticipation of any application from the State Department, as well for the purpose of placing Surratt in safe custody, as with the view to show the disposition of the Papal government to comply with the expected request of the American authorities. I have no reason to doubt the entire good faith of the Papal government in the matter.

I enclose, for the information of the department, copies of one or two additional reports upon the facts connected with Surratt's arrest and escape. With great respect, your obedient servant,

RUFUS KING.

Hon. WILLIAM H. SEWARD, *Secretary of State.*

JUAVI PONTIFICI, COMMAND OF BATTALION, Velletri, Nov. 9, 1866.

My General—Following out your excellency's orders, I sent this morning, to Veroli, Lieutenant de Farnel, to make examination into the escape of Zouave Watson. I have learned some other details of this unfortunate business. Watson, at the moment when he was arrested, must have been on his guard, having obtained knowledge of a letter addressed ——, which concerned him, probably. This letter, sent by mistake to a trumpeter named ——, was opened by him, and shown to Watson, because it was written in English. I have sent it to your eminence, with the report of Captain Lambilly.

I am assured that the escape of Watson savors of a prodigy. He leaped from a height of twenty-three feet on a very narrow rock, beyond which is a precipice. The filth from the barracks accumulated on the rock, and in this manner the fall of Watson was broken. Had he leaped a little further, he would have fallen into an abyss.

I am, with respect, my general, your eminence's humble subordinate,

ALLET, *Lieut. Col. Commanding Battalion.*

[No. 1, enclosed to Minister of War Roux.]

FEROLI, November 8.

My Colonel—I regret to announce to you that, notwithstanding all my precautions, I learn Watson has succeeded in escaping. To carry out the orders received, I had sent Sergeant Halyerid and six men to Tresulte, where this Zouave was on detachment. They did not find him there, for on that day Watson had asked leave to go to Feroli. I charged the corporal of the third company, Vanderstroeten, to take him and turn him over to the post corporal, Warrin, to whom I had already given all my instructions on this subject.

All the measures ordered were carried out from point to point. Two sentinels with loaded arms were placed—one at the very door of his prison—with orders to prevent any communication of the prisoner with persons outside, and the other at the door of the barrack. The prison, the doors and windows, &c., had been inspected in the minutest details by the locksmith of the commune. There was, therefore, nothing to fear in that quarter. All passed off well until this morning at four o'clock.

Then the prisoner was awakened, who rose, put on his gaiters, and took his coffee with a calmness and phlegm quite English. The gate of the prison opens on a platform which overlooks the country; a balustrade prevents promenaders from tumbling on the rocks, situate at least thirty-five feet below the windows of the prison.

Beside the gate of this prison are situated the privies of the barrack. Watson asked permission to halt there. Corporal Warrin, who had six men with him as guards, allowed him to stop, very naturally. nothing doubting, either he or the zouaves present, that their prisoner was going to try to escape at a place which it seemed quite impossible to us to clear. This perilous leap was, however, to be taken, to be crowned with success. In fact, Watson, who seemed quiet, seized the balustrade, made a leap, and cast himself into the void, falling on the uneven rocks, where he might have broken his bones a thousand times, and gained the depths of the valley. Patrols were immediately organized, but in vain. We saw a peasant, who told us that he had seen an unarmed zouave who was going towards Casa Mari, which is the way to Piedmont.

I address to you herewith the report of the corporal of the post, besides two letters which are not without importance. They may be of some use to the police.

Lieutenant Mously and I have been to examine the localities, and we asked ourselves how one could make such leaps without breaking arms and legs.

Please, my colonel, to receive the assurance of my respect.

DE LAMBILLY, *Commander of Detachment.*

I have sent the description of this zouave to the gens d'armerie.

Mr. King to Mr. Seward.

LEGATION OF UNITED STATES AT ROME, Nov. 20, 1866.

Sir—I have received a letter from our consul at Naples, of which I enclose a copy. I have telegraphed the information to our consul at Alexandria.

I am, sir, very respectfully, your obedient servant,

RUFUS KING.

Hon. WILLIAM H. SEWARD, *Secretary of State.*

UNITED STATES CONSULATE, Naples, Nov. 18, 1866.

Sir—I received your despatch this morning about 8 o'clock. I immediately had the police at Naples and the small towns about here hunting for Surratt, and learned, about 2 o'clock, that he left last evening at 9 o'clock, on the steamer Tripoli, for Alexandria, under the name of Walters. The steamer stops to-morrow at Malta to take in 300 tons of coal, and as the quarantine is in force there, he cannot get on shore. I immediately sent the following despatch to the consul at Malta.

"Surratt, one of the conspirators against Lincoln, left here last evening on the steamer Tripoli for Alexandria, under the name of Walters or Watson. He has on the uniform of a zouave of the Papal states. The steamer stops at Malta to-morrow to coal; have him arrested. If you do not receive this in time, telegraph the consul at Alexandria."

I did not telegraph to Alexandria, as I thought there would be plenty of time for you to do so if you thought best after the receipt of this. If our consul is in Malta, there is little doubt but he will catch him there.

Surratt has been about Naples in his zouave uniform some days. Passed himself at the British consulate as a Canadian, and was taken on this steamer through the influence of the consul.

I have the honor to be very truly yours.

FRANK SWAN, *Consul.*

Hon. RUFUS KING, *Minister, Rome.*

Mr. Seward to Mr. King.

[No. 44]   DEPARTMENT OF STATE, Washington, Nov. 26, 1866.

Sir—Your despatch, No. 65, of the 2d instant, has been received. The course which you adopted with reference to John H. Surratt is approved. We await the identification of that person. A letter of credit in your favor ——— is herewith enclosed. For the expenses which may be incurred in the case of Surratt you will draw on the Messrs. Barings ——. It is probable that a war vessel will be ordered to receive that person for transportation to this country.

I am, sir, your obedient servant,

WILLIAM H. SEWARD.

RUFUS KING, Esq.

Mr. Seward to Mr. King.

[No. 47.]   DEPARTMENT OF STATE, Washington, Nov. 30, 1866.

Sir—I have the honor to acknowledge the receipt of your despatch of November 10, No. 66. It is a subject of sincere regret that John H. Surratt effected his escape from the Papal guard. Your proceedings in communicating on that subject so promptly with Mr. Marsh, at Florence, are approved and commended. It is hoped that Surratt's re-arrest may be effected. In that expectation I shall lose no time in communicating, through that minister, with the Italian government at Florence. You cannot express too strongly to Cardinal Antonelli the satisfaction of the President with the friendly and prompt proceedings of the Papal government.   I am, sir, your obedient servant,

                                    WILLIAM H. SEWARD.
RUFUS KING, Esq.

Mr. Hale to Mr. Seward.

                        OFFICE U. S. MILITARY TELEGRAPH, Time 6.15 P. M.
[Telegram received at War Department, Washington, D. C., Dec. 2, 1866, from
                        cable, Dec. 2, 1866.]

To SEWARD, *Washington:*

Have arrested John Surratt, one of President Lincoln's assassins. No doubt of identity.

                                    HALE, *Alexandria.*

Telegram of Mr. Seward to Mr. Hale.

                        DEPARTMENT OF STATE, Washington, Dec. 3, 1866.

Sir—Your course in regard to Surratt is approved. Measures will be taken for bringing him to the United States, of which you will be advised.

          I am, sir, your obedient servant,

                                    WILLIAM H. SEWARD.
CHARLES HALE, *Consul General, Alexandria, Egypt.*

Mr. Seward to Mr. Hale.

[No. 25.]   DEPARTMENT OF STATE, Washington, Dec. 4, 1866.

Sir—The Secretary of the Navy has instructed Admiral Goldsborough to send a proper national armed vessel to Alexandria to receive from you John H. Surratt, a citizen of the United States, who is in your custody as an arrested fugitive, charged with the crime of assassination of the late Abraham Lincoln, President of the United States, and of an attempt to assassinate William H. Seward, Secretary of State of the United States, in the month of April, 1865. You will deliver the before-named to the commanding officer of the vessel upon his reporting to you his arrival at Alexandria.

          I am, sir, your obedient servant,

                                    WILLIAM H. SEWARD.
Mr. CHARLES HALE, *Alexandria, Egypt.*

Mr. Seward to Mr. Welles.

DEPARTMENT OF STATE, Washington, Dec. 4, 1866.

Sir—I give you, for your information, a copy of a despatch, which I have this day addressed to Charles Hale, Esq., consul general to Alexandria, Egypt. It is thought expedient that the prisoner, John H. Surratt, should be brought directly to the city of Washington, and delivered to the custody of the marshal of the District of Columbia, without stopping at any intermediate port either in this country or elsewhere.

I have the honor to be your obedient servant,

WILLIAM H. SEWARD.

Hon. GIDEON WELLES, *Secretary of the Navy.*

Mr. Seward to Mr. King.

[No. 49.]   DEPARTMENT OF STATE, Washington, Dec. 4, 1866.

Sir—We have telegraphic information from Mr. Hale, United States consul general at Alexandria, of the arrest of John H. Surratt there In consequence of this, Admiral Goldsborough has been ordered to send a war vessel thither for the purpose of bringing the prisoner here for trial. It is desirable and important that ———, to whom you have referred in your despatches, should also be sent hither as a witness. You will consequently apply for his discharge, ——— and, if the application should be granted, you will forward him hither. A credit for ———, touching the Surratt case, with which you have already been provided, will, it is presumed be enough to defray the expenses incident to the execution of this instruction, including the travelling expenses of ———.

I am, sir, your obedient servant,

WILLIAM H. SEWARD.

RUFUS KING, *Rome.*

Mr. F. W. Seward to Mr Dudley.

[No. 562.]   DEPARTMENT OF STATE, Washington, Dec. 6, 1866.

Sir—With Mr. Wilding's despatch No. 538, of the 27th of September, 1865, he transmitted a copy of an affidavit of ———, which represents that he was a passenger with John H. Surratt in the steamer ——— from Quebec, which arrived at Liverpool on the 25th of that month ; that, in the course of the voyage, he had conversations with Surratt, which showed that he was more or less implicated in the conspiracy which resulted in the assassination of the late President Lincoln, and perhaps in the assassination itself. Mr. Wilding says that he had ascertained that —— was ——.

As it is probable that Surratt will soon be brought to this country for trial, it would be desirable to have ——— as a witness. You will consequently try to ascertain where he now may be, and whether he would be willing to testify upon the occasion referred to.

I am, sir, your obedient servant,

F. W. SEWARD, *Assistant Secretary.*

THOMAS H. DUDLEY, *Consul, Liverpool.*

Mr. Seward to Mr. King.

[No. 50.]   DEPARTMENT OF STATE, Washington, Dec. 8, 1866.

Sir—The commanding officer of the European squadron has been instructed to station one of his vessels at Civita Vecchia, if it can be done without detriment to other important interests.

I am, sir, your obedient servant,

WILLIAM H. SEWARD.

RUFUS KING, Esq., &c., Rome.

Mr. Seward to Mr. Marsh.

[No. 160.]   DEPARTMENT OF STATE, Washington, Dec. 10, 1866.

Sir—Your despatch, No. 168, dated Nov. 18, has been received.

The course pursued by you on receiving from Mr. King, at Rome, information of the escape into Italian territory, of John H. Surratt, is approved; and the promptness and energy of your efforts to secure his re-arrest and his surrender to the United States, in the event of his being found within the Italian kingdom, are highly commended. You are, no doubt, already aware of the criminal's flight to Alexandria, and of his arrest there at the instance of the consul general, Mr. Hale.

I am, sir, your obedient servant,

WILLIAM H. SEWARD.

GEO. P. MARSH, Esq., Florence.

Mr. Seward to Mr. Harvey.

[No. 206.]   DEPARTMENT OF STATE, Washington, Dec. 10, 1866.

Sir—I have received your despatch of November 17, No. 414. Your proceedings in the matter to which it relates are approved.

I am, sir, your obedient servant,

WILLIAM H. SEWARD.

JAMES E. HARVEY, Esq., Lisbon.

SURRATT'S LAST FLIGHT AND FINAL ARREST.

WHEN the smuggler's felucca, in which Surratt had taken passage, got well out of the bay of Naples, she stood for the path usually followed by vessels bound for Malta, and was soon after overtaken by a steamer which her captain hailed, saying he had a passenger aboard who had important despatches for the British consul at Malta, and who desired to come aboard the steamer. The latter vessel at once slackened her speed, while Surratt, entering the small boat, was rowed to her side. The captain of the steamer, eager for the passage money, philosophically concluded that the stranger's business was none of his business, and therefore did not trouble him with any inquisitive questions.

Aboard the steamer, Surrattt not only failed to conceal himself, but made himself quite agreeable, and, on one or two occasions during the passage, nearly acknowledged who he really was to several persons. On nearing the island, Surratt's caution seemed to return to him, for though he believed himself safe, still he suddenly wished to make it sure. He therefore left the steamer and got aboard a small coasting sloop which would reach the wharf before the steamer, on account of the delay to the latter at the quarantine and custom station.

He was soon after landed, and was rather startled, as he walked along, to hear two men talking about himself.

" Oh," said one to the other, " we'll catch Surratt certain, for Marsh telegraphed that he had sailed on one or the other of those two steamers. Ha ! ha ! ha ! that's the time the rogue was too quick for his own good."

" Yes," was the reply, " but he may even yet give us the slip."

" Never fear," said the first. " I tell you we've got every iota arranged, and we'll have him ten minutes after he comes ashore."

The conspirator waited to hear no more, but hurried to the office of the British governor, to whom he told a piteous tale, and claimed his protection. This, so far as the law would allow him, the latter promised to extend to the fugitive, who, going straight to the office of the Malta and Alexandria steamers, took passage for the latter place, and was again at sea ere night set in.

Yet the United States consul at Malta was not thus easily thwarted, for he had already ascertained that Surratt was ashore, and at once demanded his arrest at the hands of the British governor. Had the governor chosen to do so, Surratt could have been taken at Malta. But instead, he allowed the consul's communication to lie unnoticed on his table until Surratt had sailed for Alexandria, and then the only reply he vouchsafed was that the persons alluded to had escaped.

Stung to the quick by this behavior, the U. S. consul resolved to telegraph to Charles Hale, Esq., U. S. Consul General at Alexandria, inform him of the expected appearance there of Surratt, and how he had been used by the British governor.

Consul Hale, who, from the fine likeness we give of him, will be recognized as a man of determination, resolved that nothing should thwart *him* if in his power to prevent it. So he quickly made his preparations for seizing the fugitive himself.

In due time the steamer arrived, and with several trusty Egyptian servants, Mr. Hale took a position from which, while being himself concealed, he could watch the motions of the expected conspirator. He had already received the intelligence that Surratt was still dressed in the zouave costume in which he had escaped, not having been able to obtain any different suit. Shrewdly enough, however, he did not trust to this alone, but more to the photograph which, by chance, he had in his possession.

The vessel had nearly disembarked all her passengers, and Mr. Hale began to become uneasy lest, after all his precautions, Surratt had given him the slip and already gone ashore, either among the other passengers, or by taking a boat lower down the river. But he was pleasantly reassured, when, a minute or so later, he beheld a man come up out of the companion hatchway who wore a zouave costume, and whose features answered exactly to those of the photograph.

"'Thank heaven, there's my man!" said the Consul to himself; "and I will wager my head that no British governor nor consul shall trifle with me about him."

Mr. Hale, though so desirous of at once seizing his prisoner, did not allow his anxiety destroy his judgment. He, therefore, contented himself with watching Surratt for the present, in hopes that he would stroll up by his office, when he intended to capture him and take him immediately into the office. Once there he could laugh at any efforts to release him.

Surratt, after walking the deck a few minutes, and contemplating the scenery round about, leisurely came ashore, and, unsuspectingly enough, passed directly by the ambush of Consul Hale.

There are three main streets in the ancient city of Alexandria, on which the whole population are always to be found, as a general thing, except in exceedingly bad weather. From his manner, Mr. Hale was perfectly satisfied that Surratt supposed himself entirely unknown, and was, therefore, not looking out for any peril. The consul felt that in this respect, success was almost certain, and he consequently experienced considerable relief from his previous anxiety. Still, he abated not his caution.

When the conspirator had got a short distance ahead, Mr. Hale instructed the oldest and most trusty of his Egyptian servants to follow him, engage him in conversation, and endeavor to draw him to that part of the town in which it was desirable to have him. The servant executed his mission with surprising tact and success. Running across some half submerged fields, he made a detour, by which, always keeping Surratt in sight, be could meet instead of overtake him. Pheroda—for such was the servant's name— argued, and correctly too, that to meet the intended captive would certainly not excite suspicion, while to overtake him might.

"How do, solger mans?" said Pheroda, accosting Surratt, and making a low obeisance; "how do? I poor—I work for you."

Surratt, never suspecting any design in the innocent looking native, inspected him for a few moments, as he might have done an ox or horse, and then said, in a tone intended to be impressive:

"Well, you talk pretty good English, and I want a good servant. What's your name?"

"Phedora. I learn Englicha by the men on the ships. I talk Englicha goods. I make good serve; bring you water; I hew your wood."

"Well, Pheroda," replied Surratt, as the Egyptian, with another low salaam, awaited what he should say, "you would suit me excellently, I believe, provided I can trust you; and, egad, ha! ha! ha! the only treasure I can trust you with is myself. But, I say, old Pharaoh, Ptolemy, or what- ever you call yourself, if you knew what a pearl of great price I am, and what I would bring to the lucky finder, it wouldn't do to trust you—not much! But, jokes aside, Pheroda, I want a servant here, until I start for Abyssinia. What will you serve me faithfully for?"

Pheroda, who understood every word Surratt uttered, though the con- spirator little thought so, named an exceedingly small sum, and was imme- diately engaged. Telling his new master that he had to do an errand close at hand, but that he would speedily overtake him, Pheroda left Surratt, and in a short space of time was communicating his success, so far, to Mr. Hale. The consul, delighted with the Egyptian, bade him return to Surratt, and guide him near a ruined hut that stood close in the rear of the con- sulate.

Pheroda promptly went back to the conspirator, who began to ply him with questions as to the residences of the French, British, and American consuls, what kind of men they were, &c. The wily Egyptian was always ready with a reply, and several times excited the merriment of Surratt, who, apparently indifferent, suffered his new servant to guide him as he pleased.

In the meantime, Mr. Hale, with two of the other servants, bearing manacles, hurried to the rear of the ruined hut, where he awaited the ap- pearance of Surratt. At last he saw him, and a thrill of joy passed through him, as he drew his pistol and carefully examined the cap. For he had reasoned, that as Surratt was such a desperate man, it would be only placing his own life in peril, not to be fully armed when he should attempt to make the arrest.

On came the two travelers, until they were directly opposite the hut. At this juncture, Pheroda, uttering an exclamation of surprise, darted away into some clumps of bushes which grew on the opposite side of the path to where Mr. Hale was concealed.

This ruse of Pheroda's succeeded most admirably in its object, which was to cause Surratt to turn his back to his intended captor, and thus give the latter the advantage of a full surprise.

Mr. Hale saw it instantly, and as Surratt wheeled to look in wonderment at his servant's unaccountable motion, the consul sprang upon him from his ambush, and seizing him by the shoulder, while he held the revolver at his head—

"You are John Surratt!" he said, in a determined tone. "Surrender yourself my prisoner, in the name of the United States Government, which I represent. Ah! do not draw that dagger!" he continued, as the astounded Surratt grasped at the haft of the weapon. "It is useless. One movement, and I will shoot you! Do you surrender?"

Surratt, trembling excessively, after a slight hesitation, replied:
" Yes."

" Ho, there, bring those manacles!" called out Mr. Hale to the two servants, never taking his pistol down, however, nor relaxing his iron grip on his prisoner.

"Don't put them on me, I'll go along peaceably," pleaded the captive, at the same time handing his weapons to his captor, who granted his request, but kept his pistol ready for use at any instant, while marching Surratt into his house, in a secure room of which he was soon afterward imprisoned.

This accomplished, Consul Hale notified the Egyptian government of his procedure, and demanded the necessary authority to hold and remove his prisoner, whenever he should receive instructions from Secretary Seward. The Pashaw promptly and courteously acceded to the demand; and Mr. Hale at once sent home to Washington the laconic despatch:

"*I have arrested John H. Surratt—no question of identity.*"

Now that the capture was made certain, it became necessary that the prisoner should be brought to the United States for trial. And the importance and peculiarity surrounding the case demanded some special attention to the subject of the manner in which the captive conspirator should be conveyed.

After considerable thought and consultation between Secretary Seward and other high government officials, it was finally agreed among them to adhere to the original programme which had been fixed upon when the intelligence reached Washington that Surratt had been arrested in Italy. This was to dispatch a United States steam vessel of war, have the prisoner placed on board, and landed directly at Washington city.

Accordingly, Mr. Seward sent a telegram by the Atlantic cable to his subordinate, to have the matter thus arranged. In obedience to this order the Swatara was detached from Admiral Goldsborough's squadron, in the Mediterranean, and sent to Alexandria, there to report to Consul-General Hale. All orders were executed promptly, and the steamer, toward the latter part of December, steamed up the Nile, came to, off the ancient city of Alexandria, and was duly reported to Mr. Hale, who at once marched Surratt, well guarded, on board.

In a reported conversation between the Consul and a friend of his, the former expressed the deepest relief from a terrible anxiety, which possessed him up to the moment he surrendered his charge into the care of the Swatara's captain. For Surratt had hitherto been so successful in escaping, where escape seemed impossible, as much on account of the material aid he received from British and other consuls and officials—notwithstanding they really knew who he was—as from his own good fortune and desperation, that he dreaded each morning getting up and finding the bird flown.

This time, however, Fate decided against the fugitive, who had thus for so long a time baffled all attempts to take him, and Surratt, after wandering up and down the earth with the mark of Cain upon his brow, was at last going home, not to meet the pleasant greeting of friends, nor the loving embrace of a mother, for of the former he had none, and the latter he had allowed to die ignominiously on the scaffold, when, by suffering death himself he might have saved her life. Never was a human being more alone in this world than is John H. Surratt to-day.

Many are the surmises as to what will be his fate; but of course, it is useless to speculate as to that, for if there be proof to show his connection with this great crime, for which his mother, in company with Payne, Harold and Atzerott, suffered the extremest penalty of the law, there can exist no doubt that he will suffer the self-same doom as they did.

The unfortunate Louise Le Grande, finding she had been so contemptibly treated by the conspirator, could not survive her sorrow and shame. She therefore sent her servant to bring a brazier and some charcoal, under the plea of coldness, and, shutting herself in her chamber, she lit the fatal fire, threw herself on the bed, and was found the next morning a corpse.

www.ingramcontent.com/pod-product-compliance
Lightning Source LLC
Chambersburg PA
CBHW021226260626
47172CB00002B/628